DOUBLE PLAY

BE A GENIUS!
READ THE FIRST BOOK.
Baseball Genius

BASEBALL GENIUS
DOUBLE PLAY

TIM GREEN · DEREK JETER

JETER CHILDREN'S

ALADDIN

New York London Toronto Sydney New Delhi

ALADDIN
An imprint of Simon & Schuster Children's Publishing Division
1230 Avenue of the Americas, New York, New York 10020
First Aladdin hardcover edition March 2018
Text copyright © 2018 by Tim Green
Jacket illustration copyright © 2018 by Tim Jessell
All rights reserved, including the right of reproduction
in whole or in part in any form.
ALADDIN and related logo are registered trademarks of Simon & Schuster, Inc.
For information about special discounts for bulk purchases, please contact
Simon & Schuster Special Sales at 1-866-506-1949 or business@simonandschuster.com.
The Simon & Schuster Speakers Bureau can bring authors to your live event.
For more information or to book an event contact the Simon & Schuster Speakers
Bureau at 1-866-248-3049 or visit our website at www.simonspeakers.com.
Jacket designed by Jessica Handelman
Interior designed by Mike Rosamilia
The text of this book was set in Centennial LT Std.
Manufactured in the United States of America 0218 FFG
2 4 6 8 10 9 7 5 3 1
Library of Congress Cataloging-in-Publication Data
Names: Green, Tim, 1963- author. | Jeter, Derek, 1974- author.
Title: Double play / Tim Green, Derek Jeter.
Description: First Aladdin hardcover edition. | New York : Aladdin, 2018. |
Series: Baseball genius ; [2] | Summary: When New York Yankee James "JY" Yager
strikes out on his own to show he can still hit in the majors without the help of
twelve-year-old Jalen's baseball genius, Jalen focuses on his own baseball career
as he tries to carve out a spot with the Rockton Rockets.
Identifiers: LCCN 2017045564 | ISBN 9781534406681 (hc) |
ISBN 9781534406704 (eBook)
Subjects: | CYAC: Baseball—Fiction. | Racially mixed people—Fiction. |
BISAC: JUVENILE FICTION / Sports & Recreation / Baseball & Softball. |
JUVENILE FICTION / Social Issues / Friendship. | JUVENILE FICTION / Family /
General (see also headings under Social Issues).
Classification: LCC PZ7.G826357 Do 2018 | DDC [Fic]—dc23
LC record available at https://lccn.loc.gov/2017045564

*For my son, Ty—strong, smart,
and, best of all, kind*
—T. G.

*To Bella, who can become
anything she wants*
—D. J.

1

THE POLICEMAN TIGHTENED HIS GRIP ON JALEN'S
arm.

Jalen just grinned.

Up they went in a fancy elevator reserved for the Yankee Stadium VIPs. Down a hallway lined with team offices, all lit up. People bustling by gave them curious glances. Jalen supposed the offices stayed busy into the night when there was a game, and there *had* been a game, another victory for the Yankees.

Jalen's grin was born from something bigger than a win, even though the Yankees were his team. His was the grin of someone whose life was about to change. Someone who'd won the lottery or unexpectedly inherited a fortune from a long-lost relative. It was the smile of the kid who'd gotten the lead role in a play, or the MVP trophy at the team banquet. He wanted to share his joy, and he wished the policeman would ease up on his arm.

"Everyone looks happy about the game." Jalen smiled up at him, but the massive officer remained stone-faced. Of course, how could the policeman have known that Jalen's ability to predict the next pitch in an MLB game—or any game, for that matter—had helped the Yankees *win* this one?

They stopped outside a pair of dark, tall wooden doors. Jalen thought the officer was reaching for one of the heavy chrome handles, but instead he knocked. After a moment, he knocked again and a stern voice ordered them inside. The Yankees GM, Jeffrey Foxx, sat behind a mahogany desk which was as broad as a boat. A telephone was pressed against his ear. Foxx pointed, not to the chairs, but to an empty space on the thick rug in front of the desk as he finished his call.

"You never were good at poker, Don," Foxx said. "You're bluffing, and I'm going to double down. Good luck."

The GM hung up the phone with anger in his eyes. Even though Foxx was sitting behind a desk, Jalen felt his power.

The policeman finally let Jalen loose. He flashed a

smile up at the officer while rubbing the blood back into his arm.

"Thanks, Jimmy," the GM said to the cop. "You can wait outside."

Suddenly Jalen hated to see the enormous policeman go.

"How about you take those sunglasses off so I can see you?" Foxx hadn't blinked.

Jalen had forgotten about his glasses. He removed his hat and pushed them up onto his dark, curly hair. His eyes adjusted to the brightly lit office. In the window behind the desk, the stadium lights burned white and the empty field glowed emerald-green, a rare bit of color in the concrete city.

"Those were so no one could see what you were up to, right?" The GM's frown deepened.

Jalen adjusted the glasses. "I guess."

"You guess." Without warning, the GM smacked his hand down on the top of the desk with a noise like the crack of an ax.

Jalen jumped.

Foxx leaned forward, planting his hands on the desk as if he was preparing to pounce. His voice was a low, nasty growl. "Son, I have no idea why you're standing there smiling. You are in a *world* of trouble."

2

JALEN'S SMILE CRUMPLED.

"Do you think what you were doing is okay?" Foxx waved his hands toward the stadium behind him. "For a twelve-year-old kid to steal signs in a major league game? Did you think I was going to sing your praises for helping James Yager save his career?"

"Well . . . it worked." Jalen felt a tremor in his voice and his mouth dried like dust. "You won, right? That's what you want. That's what everyone wants."

"Without *cheating*." The GM smacked the desk again. "If I was going to cheat, I certainly wouldn't do it with a snot-nosed kid. Now, you've already stolen from this stadium, you've trespassed in this stadium, and we can add cheating in this stadium to the list."

Jalen tried to swallow. His father would kill him for stealing, and it hadn't felt like stealing when he did it. "It was just some dirt."

"Dirt you were told to return. Dirt you got from going out onto the field when you had no right to do so. Do you know what they do with boys who commit crimes? Boys from broken homes?"

"My home's not broken," Jalen somehow managed to say, even though the defiance he felt didn't sound as serious as he intended.

"Oh, no? A mother who married your dad so he could get a green card, then poof, she just disappears? Sounds pretty messed up to me."

Jalen felt like he'd been slapped.

"Yeah, I know all about you."

Jalen narrowed his eyes, thinking hard.

"Chris." The name came—and the twitch in Foxx's grin told him he was right. Chris Gamble was a brute, a big jerk who happened to be a teammate and classmate of Jalen's.

"It doesn't matter how I know," Foxx continued, "but I know."

"I didn't steal any signs." Jalen raised his chin. "I don't have to."

Foxx snorted. "Oh, really? What do you do? Read a crystal ball?"

Jalen bit his tongue. James Yager had insisted that he not tell anyone how he did what he did. It was nearly impossible to explain anyway—a hurricane of numbers and intuitions flashing across his brain. Jalen curled his lower lip up under his top teeth.

"Nothing, huh?" Foxx sneered. "How about I give you a little push in the right direction? See, I know what this is all about . . . all this talk about lucky calamari and some grand reopening of your father's restaurant—a guy who doesn't have two nickels to rub together, a man who can't pay his bills one week to the next. You steal the signs to help Yager, and he tweets and whatever else he does to get his fans—my *team's* fans—to flock to this crummy little diner in Rockton. I know exactly what's going on, I just don't know *how*, and that's where you come in.

"You're going to tell me how this whole thing works, and then I'm going to expose Yager for the fraud he is. I'll put him on the waiver wire. Maybe Los Angeles or San Francisco will pick up half his salary. I'll eat the rest to get rid of him."

Jalen couldn't believe the GM's smile as he said, "The

Yankees will move on with my new prospect—a kid who'll be better than Yager by July."

That gave Jalen a jolt, but he reminded himself of just how popular JY really was. He might be toward the end of his career, but he was adored, and not just by Yankees fans. Any fan of baseball had a soft spot for JY, an all-around good guy with an all-star résumé.

"People won't let you do that," Jalen said hotly.

"Oh, no?" The GM leaned back, cracked a knuckle, and folded his hands together. "You haven't seen my guy! And think about how your father is gonna feel when I press charges against you." Foxx ground his teeth. "You might think, 'Oh, I'm just a kid,' but this isn't Rockton. You can bet I know plenty of police like Jimmy, and plenty of judges."

Jalen's mouth fell open. It didn't seem possible, but when he spoke, it came out as weak as a kitten's whimper. "You can't do that."

"Oh, yes." Foxx's smile grew. "Oh, yes I can."

Just then, without warning, the office door flew open.

3

JAMES YAGER STILL WORE HIS UNIFORM, SPIKES
and all. Only his hat was missing, and his brown eyes were
bright with anger and emotion.

Foxx stood up behind his desk. "You don't just barge
in here."

"You don't hold a twelve-year-old kid against his will,"
Yager shot right back, and the words hit home.

Foxx sputtered. "He's . . . I'm trying to determine whether
or not to have him arrested and press charges."

"Charges?" JY shot a look at Jalen, then put a protec-
tive hand on his shoulder.

In the doorway, Jalen saw the faces of his friends, Cat

and Daniel, along with Cat's mom, and the giant policeman towering over them.

"Trespassing," said the GM, nodding at the officer, who nodded back. "Stealing."

JY snorted. "There're two dozen reporters downstairs wanting to see the kid with the lucky calamari. You want me to tell them he's being detained by you because he took some *dirt*? Come on, Jeffrey, look at yourself. It's over. We won, and you're gonna have to get used to me being around for a while longer."

Foxx's face flamed red. Jalen had run across his kind before—customers in his father's diner, a notorious social studies teacher who prowled the lunchroom at school. Foxx was a man used to giving orders and seeing them carried out. He was the kind of person who believed he was always right and would become furious when others didn't believe it too.

Foxx pointed a long, tan finger at JY. A thick gold bracelet drooped from his wrist. "You won't be around here for another *day*. You're done. Finished."

JY blinked, then recovered, smiling. He spoke softly and calmly. "We had a deal. Everyone knows about it. Tom Verducci quoted you on SI.com. The media's going crazy downstairs. They love it, the wily old rabbit's back in the briar patch."

Foxx smiled right back. "Right. We had a deal that if you batted a thousand in these last three games I'd extend your contract. No one thought that was possible. I looked at it as a public relations novelty—like giving out bobbleheads—to create some excitement and send you off into the sunset."

"But then I actually *did it*." Yager let go of Jalen's shoulder. He clenched his fists and jutted out his chin. "I batted a thousand. Three games in a row."

"Not quite." Foxx angled his head and his eyes flicked at Jalen. "*He* did it, by stealing signs. Cheating wasn't part of the bargain, and you know how the owner feels. Honesty means everything to Mr. Brenneck. And the media? They're a pack of jackals. They'll snap up whatever scraps you fling at them. A cheating scandal is a lot tastier to them than a comeback story about a kid with some rubbery squid doused in ketchup. A scandal is sirloin steak to those animals."

"Yeah, except you're wrong, Jeffrey." JY put his hand back on Jalen's shoulder. "He didn't steal anyone's signs."

"And we can *prove* it." Everyone's eyes turned toward Cat. She had marched herself into the office and stood only a pace behind JY.

Foxx laughed out loud at her. "You think anyone cares about what some goofy kids say? You think Mr. Brenneck is going to listen to a word anyone says over me?"

"I sure do." Cat's blue eyes sparkled with confidence.

She held her head straight and, like her mom, was so pretty that she unnerved most people.

Foxx wasn't most people, though, and he snickered.

Cat looked back at her mom before she said, "He'll listen to my stepdad. He was Mr. Brenneck's frat brother at Yale, wasn't he, Mom? The frat was Deke or Dirk or something?"

Cat's mom drifted into the room, tall and straight and elegant in a black silk blouse and pleated cream-colored pants. She extended a hand to the GM in a casual greeting. On her other hand a rectangular diamond as wide as a dime glinted in the light. "I think we may have actually met once, Mr. Foxx. In Scotty's box."

Jalen knew that Mr. Brenneck's name was Scott, but by the look of surprise on Foxx's face, he didn't imagine many people called the owner by his first name, let alone "Scotty."

"He's such a teddy bear . . . Scotty." Cat's mom had deep blue eyes like Cat, and they seemed to glitter with glee. "I'm certain he'll at least give us a chance to explain. Maybe you should too? I only mention it to be polite."

Foxx looked like he was choking on a fishbone. His face turned colors, and no words came out. Finally he managed to scowl and speak. "And just *how* is this kid helping JY without stealing signs?"

"Tell him, amigo!" Daniel barked at Jalen from the

doorway, where he still stood in the shadow of the policeman. "My man is a *baseball genius*."

"Oh, *really?*" Foxx's scowl deepened.

Jalen knew the GM was quite proud that people sometimes referred to *him* as a genius. Foxx was one of the youngest GMs in major league baseball, and many people attributed the rapid rise to his smarts.

"Yeah, he really is. He can tell you what the next pitch is gonna be!" Daniel waved his hands in the air. Spit flew from his mouth, and he didn't seem to notice the GM's displeasure. "He doesn't need signs. He just *knows*. My man, he's just a *genius!*"

"So!" Foxx raised his voice, staring at JY now. "You admit that this kid told you the pitches?"

"He did." JY nodded. "To help me out of my slump."

"And when I had him in Girardi's office, he used his phone to call this young lady." Foxx pointed at Cat. "And she flashed you some secret code?"

"Yes, when you had him locked up." JY scowled. "That's how we did it."

Foxx smiled a toothy smile and angled his head at the officer in the doorway. "Now I have a witness. You admitted it."

"Jalen told me the pitches," JY said. "So?"

"So, *that is cheating!* And you, James Yager, are *finished*." Foxx thumped his hand on the desk.

4

"THAT IS *NOT* CHEATING," YAGER SAID, NOT sounding entirely confident.

"Oh, but it is," said Foxx. "That's worse than stealing signs. You used electronics to convey the information. *That* is specifically against the established rules. There was a memo from the MLB chief of operations in 2000 prohibiting the use of electronic devices to convey information that gives any club an advantage.

"So, you were cheating." Foxx grinned wider still. Then his face dropped in mock seriousness. "We may have to forfeit the game. Probably the only decent thing to do."

"We didn't *need* the phones. We only used them because you had Jalen locked up." Cat pointed a finger at the GM.

BASEBALL GENIUS

"He was sequestered, not locked up," said Foxx. "And that was the New York City Police, not me. It was that or take him to the station. I think I was being a sport by allowing them to keep him in Joe's office. Either way, James, I think you see this is over. Best for all if you stand down and retire with some grace. What a send-off, right? Batting a thousand and winning your final game with a two-run RBI? Doesn't get much better."

"So you'd overlook the whole thing with the phones?" JY asked. "Because you really don't care about that."

"Why make things messy? Say you want to retire and go peacefully." Foxx raised his eyebrows. "I respect you, James, for what you've given for this club. It's just that it's time. You know it, I know it, and I'm sure Mr. Brenneck agrees. It's about the numbers."

JY tilted his head and spoke softly. "I gave you numbers, Jeffrey."

"But it wasn't *you*." The GM spoke just as softly, and he nodded at Jalen. "It was him, and he can't be there for you every game."

"Oh yes, he can!" Cat announced. "JY and I already have a deal. School ends next week, and Jalen can help out all summer."

Jalen's head snapped around. They had *talked* about putting some kind of a deal together, but it was all just an

14

idea. Cat was bluffing, but JY wasn't giving anything away either, so Jalen stayed quiet.

"So, we're back to whether or not you want to give Jalen the chance to show how he can do this without stealing signs," JY said. "Because if he can do it without seeing the catcher give a sign and then let me know what pitch is coming with a simple hand gesture, it isn't breaking any rules at all. It won't create even the hint of a problem, because he's not stealing signs."

No one moved. The room remained silent until there was a scuffle in the hallway and a young woman in a skirt appeared, with messy long hair and dark-framed glasses that had somehow gone crooked on her face. She slipped past the policeman into the room and pointed at Jalen. "Boss, I'm sorry, but we really need this kid. The press is making all kinds of noise."

"Hi, Glenda," JY said pleasantly, and it was obvious he knew the woman well. "I was just telling Jeffrey that."

"Yeah, they're bonkers down there." She chuckled and smiled at JY before blowing a strand of hair from her face with a puff. "Whew."

"The press!" The GM glowered.

"Uh . . . Boss, I was just . . . letting you know. They, uh . . . Okay." The woman straightened her glasses and turned to go.

"Wait!" Foxx gave a deep sigh. "Take him. Go. All of you. Out of my sight." He pointed at the door.

"So, we're good?" JY asked. "You're giving me my extension?"

Foxx spoke so low Jalen could barely hear him. "I am not good, and I have no idea whether or not I'm giving you an extension. That depends on a lot of things."

Foxx got louder. "No, you go have your press conference. Say whatever you want, but from me, it'll be 'No comment.' Let's just see how you make out.

"Good luck, James. You're gonna need it."

5

"WHAT ARE YOU GOING TO SAY?" JALEN ASKED AS
they rode the elevator back down.

Yager shrugged. "I'm thinking."

"I'd like it if you told them I'm . . . you know," Jalen said, "a baseball genius."

Glenda gave Jalen, then JY, a puzzled look.

JY turned away. When the elevator bell dinged, he let Glenda off before answering Jalen. "It's lucky calamari." He kept his voice low. "That's it. Just luck. Got it? Nothing else. I need to get that contract extension signed."

Jalen opened his mouth. "But—"

JY silenced him with a raised finger. "Shh. Think about this: it'll help your father, this 'lucky calamari' thing. The focus will be on his restaurant, not you. We'll promote the grand reopening tomorrow night, and people will swarm to the place for some lucky calamari. It's about your dad, right? This whole thing? That's what you said."

Jalen looked at his friends, searching for answers. Seeing himself in their eyes, he knew what he had to do.

"Okay." He couldn't help feeling and sounding glum.

Glenda led them to the media room, where JY and Jalen stepped up onto a small stage and sat down side by side, facing a slew of camera lights and eager faces. The room exploded with questions until Glenda leaned into the microphones and held up her hand. "One at a time. One at a time. Mark, you first."

A gel-haired young man wearing a tight suit cleared his throat and asked, "JY, can you tell us who the boy is exactly, and how he's responsible for salvaging your career?"

JY smiled broadly and put a hand on Jalen's shoulder. "This is Jalen DeLuca, he's a fan, and he contacted me through some mutual friends."

JY flicked his eyes toward the doorway, where Cat stood with her mom and Daniel.

"He told me he could help me out of my slump, that his dad had this amazing dish, this stuffed calamari that'd bring me luck. Now, I had a laugh over that, but then I got to thinking, the way things were headed, why not try it? His dad's place is in Rockton, where I live, the Silver Liner Diner, right next to the train station. I like Italian food anyway, so I figured I'd give it a shot and then—bingo—I batted a thousand. Well, only a fool wouldn't keep eating that lucky calamari, so I kept at it these last three nights and . . . well, you saw how it went."

Again the room erupted in a storm of questions until Glenda repeated her call for order, then pointed to the blond woman from FOX. "Margaret?"

"Two nights ago, Jalen told me it was *him*."

"I—" Jalen began to speak, but JY kicked him under the table. "I only meant we, my dad and me, because I help him in the kitchen."

"And"—JY leaned into the microphones—"Jalen being able to come watch me play along with his friends was part of the deal. Torin, how about you? Two weeks ago I think you called me 'washed up.' How about now?"

The handsome gray-haired man who'd first called Jalen "Calamari Kid" blushed before he said, "Looked that way, but not anymore. You saved your career! How does that feel?"

"How does it feel?" JY leaned back in his chair and took a deep breath and let it out slowly. His eyes filled, and it looked like he might spill a tear before he regained his composure. "It's like that car crash that almost kills you and you pull over and you realize how close you came and you're just flooded with . . . joy? Gratitude?

"Let me make something clear. I came up with the Yankees. I turned twos with Jeter and played behind Mo Rivera. I'm going to go out a Yankee, like they did." Yager grinned. "It's all good, especially with lucky calamari."

The lights and the questions and the excitement dazed Jalen, so when Glenda ended it before the media was ready to stop, and he was shuffled out of the room, he couldn't recall most of what had been said. On the car ride home, he realized how tired he was, too tired to celebrate, to chatter, to even notice the diner, repairs completed and slumbering in the dark in preparation for its big day. So when Cat's mom dropped him off in front of his sagging house and he waved good-bye from the front porch, it seemed like the whole thing might have been a dream.

Inside, his father jumped up from his chair. The TV flickered on the wall.

"Jalen!" His father hugged him tight and kissed his cheeks. "I didn't hear you coming. I was watching the TV, and I did not see the lights. You friends, they go? They don't want something to eat?"

"No, Dad."

"I see you on the TV!" His father pointed to the muted flat-screen. "They're all talking about JY and about *you*."

"Not the diner?"

"Oh yeah, they talk plenty about the diner, and they say tomorrow—the grand reopening—she's gonna be like a rock concert! Everybody wanna be there. Everybody gonna be happy!" Jalen's dad put his hands on either side of Jalen's face and looked into his eyes, choking up just like JY had done at the press conference. "Jalen . . . is my dream coming true, and you're the one who's making it happen."

Jalen hugged him hard and took a deep breath. "Dad, I'm so tired. I gotta get some sleep. Remember, we gotta be at the bus by six tomorrow morning."

"What bus?"

"Dad, the tournament's tomorrow. The Rockets?"

"Oh yeah! And I gotta get the sandwiches ready." His dad slapped a hand against his bald scalp. "You go to bed. I'm gonna get everything ready, then make them in the morning so they fresh."

Originally, Coach Gamble had agreed to take Jalen onto the travel team even though he only had half the thousand-dollar fee, so long as Jalen's dad supplied sandwiches for the players when they traveled and catered the end-of-season banquet. But Cat—being the shrewd

21

negotiator she was—had gotten JY to agree not only to tweet the Silver Liner into the limelight, but also to pay the rest of Jalen's fee *if* Jalen helped him.

"Dad, JY paid Coach Gamble so you don't have to make any sandwiches."

"I know, but I wanna do that for the boys. They gonna love my sandwiches."

Jalen knew better than to argue with his father about food, so he quickly took care of business in the bathroom before flopping down in the narrow bed in the corner of his tiny room. He set his alarm for five o'clock and reached for the light switch. When his eyes caught sight of the picture on his bureau, his fingers froze. His mother's image—a beauty with big eyes, dark skin, and full red lips—smiled out into the room.

Without warning, Jalen choked up like his father and JY before him. Today had been one of the biggest days in his life, tomorrow would be another one, and with a kick that reminded him of the time he'd put a fork in the electric outlet, he suddenly missed her. He didn't just miss her presence, having a mom to come home to who baked cookies or helped with science homework. He missed her from the inside out, as if suddenly aware of an enormous empty space in his chest that just wasn't supposed to be.

He stared for quite some time at the picture, and she

stared right back, and it was as if she was calling to him and he knew—deep down—that she wanted him to find her. Something had kept them apart, and he suspected that it wasn't entirely her own doing and that she needed him to reach out. He just knew it.

And, as he switched off the light and shut his eyes, the only thing that allowed him to fall asleep was the promise that he'd find her.

6

IN THE MORNING, HE SPRANG FROM HIS BED,
slapping at the alarm until it went quiet, then bolted for
the bathroom. Somewhere between a shower and brush-
ing his teeth he really woke up, and it was his own baseball tournament that occupied his mind. The restaurant,
his friends, JY, being a baseball genius, and even the
mother he was determined to find all dropped back to the
end of the line, crowded out by thoughts of ground balls,
strikes, home runs, and double plays.

He smelled breakfast as he pulled on his uniform, so the
snap of eggs and bacon didn't surprise him as he rushed
into the kitchen. His father smelled of shaving lotion, and

he looked and moved about the kitchen like it was mid-day, not early dawn.

"There's my boy. Right on time." His father carried the hot skillet to the table and slid some breakfast onto two plates. "You eat, then you play good."

Nerves dampened Jalen's appetite, but he knew a long day should start with a good breakfast, and his father would be upset if he didn't eat, so he chewed and swallowed.

"Leave the plates," his father said. "I take you to the bus, and then I clean up."

"You've got a lot of work to do today, right?" Jalen was thinking about the grand reopening.

His father put a thumb in the center of his chest. "Is not work for me to cook. It's what I do. Is a joy."

"Like baseball," Jalen said.

"For you is like baseball. Play, not work." His dad's face glowed behind the small wire-frame glasses and his blue eyes sparkled. "You get your bag, I get the sandwiches."

"When did you make them?" Jalen asked.

"About four. I got a big day today. I'm no sleep."

"Dad, I said you didn't have to." Jalen dipped out of the kitchen and back down the short hallway to retrieve his gear bag.

His dad held the front door for him and said, "I'm think-ing about you and your team eating these sandwiches, and I'm thinking I'm gonna help you win. It's makin' me happy."

Jalen chuckled and got into the minivan. "Thanks, Dad."

Already the chill from the night air seemed to be fading, and the clear pink sky above promised a beautiful day for baseball. In that light, Jalen could make out more of the details of their home. Once a railroad shed, it had been cobbled into a small, disjointed house through the years. Even Jalen's inexpert eye could see where the bedrooms had been added, a stained blue tarp bridging the old and the new to keep water from leaking between the roof-lines. One broken window had been replaced by a board, and the porch rested crookedly on piles of cinder blocks and fieldstones. The part of the porch that once wrapped around the side had collapsed after a snowstorm, but you could still see the unpainted scars where it had been attached, and their nail holes bleeding rust. In the day-light, it was an embarrassment, and it knotted Jalen's stomach to think about one of those reporters showing up and possibly snapping a picture.

Meanwhile, Jalen realized they weren't moving. He shifted his focus to the tired-sounding engine as his father turned the key again and again before stopping with a sigh.

"I don't know. Maybe she's flooded."

Jalen looked at the clock on the dash. It read 5:43, but the school parking lot was ten minutes away. A chill, along with the words of warning Coach Gamble had given them all—*be there by six or we leave without you*—passed through his brain.

"Maybe we become a famous restaurant," his dad said as he popped the hood. He fished some tools out of the case behind the driver's seat and held up a wrench at Jalen. "Then we gonna get a new van."

His father hustled outside, raised the hood, and bent over the engine. Jalen stood beside him, willing the thing to work, but with very little idea what was happening. His father always insisted that engines weren't something he should worry about.

"You keep doing good in school," his father would say as he swished Jalen away from any mechanical projects he might be after. "You gonna be a doctor or a lawyer. You're not gonna have space in your brain for mechanics, too."

Right now Jalen wished he knew, wished he could help, but he could only stand with his hands shoved deep into his pockets and worry as time seeped away.

"Now she's gonna work!" His father wiped his hands on his pants and slammed the hood with confidence.

Jalen scurried into the passenger seat. His father got in and turned the key.

The engine groaned in a steady beat without catching fire. His father kept the key turned until the groan became a weary moan that steadily slowed before he let go.

"The battery, she's gonna die." His father stared hard at the controls. "I got maybe one more try. Maybe two."

His father suddenly slammed a hand on the dash, and Jalen did the same, even though he was pretty sure that wouldn't help the situation. The clock now read 5:49.

The reason everything in the past few days had happened was because Jalen wanted to play on the Rockets. It was the only show in town, a 13U travel team that would give him a summer of competition on the bigger field. It wasn't Little League anymore. At this stage kids began to play on a field as big as the pros used—ninety feet between the bases instead of sixty.

It was a transition Jalen knew he had to make, or be left behind forever as a young baseball player with no hope of making it to the pros. All the trouble he'd been in and out of was so he could play. Even the excitement of helping JY salvage his career, and being part of his favorite team's wins, didn't compare to how important today was to him. And, because of all that other stuff, Jalen was already on probation with his coach and had been strictly warned that if he missed this morning's bus, he was finished.

So he clenched his jaw and tried not to shout at his father. "Dad, hurry!"

His father—not a churchgoing man—did have a silver cross he wore around his neck, and at times like this, he pulled it out and kissed it before closing his eyes and turning the key once more.

7

THE ENGINE TURNED, COUGHED, CAUGHT HOLD,
and roared to life.

"Hurry," Jalen said.

They flew past the diner, and Jalen's dad couldn't help puffing up with pride.

"Look at her, Jalen," he said, "she's like-a new."

Jalen looked anxiously at the clock before looking out the window. Except for a few remaining pieces of construction equipment and some orange barrels to keep people off the newly planted grass, no one would have suspected that just a few days ago there'd been a pretty serious kitchen fire. His dad was right, the place looked like new, and in a way, it was new. All that, Jalen knew, was thanks to James Yager. But if he was being honest, JY wouldn't have gotten involved if it wasn't for Cat. She was the mastermind behind it all, the one with enough nerve to ask for—or maybe she'd actually insisted on—JY's help.

On the street leading from the school they passed drivers in various cars and SUVs heading home, having dropped their kids off on time. The clock said 5:59 when they raced up and shuddered to a halt behind the diesel fumes shrouding the bus. Jalen dashed toward Coach Gamble.

The enormous man held a clipboard in his hand.

"You just made it," Coach Gamble snorted, looking at his watch.

Jalen stepped up onto the first step of the bus, insuring he wouldn't be left behind, before turning to see his dad trundling up along the length of the bus, with the cooler in both hands weighing him down.

"Coach," Jalen's dad said brightly, "I got you sandwiches for the team. They gonna love 'em."

"What?" Coach Gamble scowled at the cooler. "Oh, I got Subway, so we're all set."

"Well, I make them, so I leave for the boys in case they want some, no?" Jalen's dad was smiling, and Jalen flared with shame. The way his father talked embarrassed him in public, so there was that shame. But he was ashamed

31

of himself, too, for wishing the father he loved wasn't so different.

"Yeah, sure. Put them underneath with the equipment. That's fine." Coach Gamble turned to Jalen. "Don't just stand there. Give your dad a hand, and stow your gear underneath too. That's how we do it. Then get on board, because we are leaving this minute."

Jalen stowed his gear bag next to the rest and helped his father slide the cooler into an empty spot before kissing him good-bye.

"You gonna have-a good luck today," his father said. "I feel it! And don't forget you sandwiches. They gonna help!"

"Bye, Dad. See you tonight for the party." Jalen boarded the bus, looking for Daniel.

The door hissed shut, and ignoring Jalen, Coach Gamble roared, "Roll it out, Bussie."

As Jalen made his way down the aisle toward the back, where he suspected Daniel would be, someone tripped him. Jalen stumbled, but caught himself and looked back to see Chris Gamble and Dirk Benning—both the coaches' sons—grinning at him.

"Did Jalen just *kiss* some bald guy?" Chris asked Dirk without taking his hateful eyes off Jalen. Chris was not only the coach's son, he also was the biggest kid in the sixth grade, by far. Even the eighth graders gave him space, so he was used to saying whatever he liked to whoever he felt like saying it to.

"Yeah, a real smoocher," Dirk said, making kissing noises with his own lips before breaking out in a hearty laugh.

An idea crossed Jalen's mind connecting Dirk's noises with Chris's gigantic butt, but he tossed that into a wastebasket of other crumpled-up insults he kept in the corner of his mind. Instead he said, "He's my *dad*."

"Oh, Daddy, kissy, kissy." Chris now made kissing noises as well.

Then Daniel appeared. He lived above the stable on the estate Cat's stepfather owned, and he never invented an insult that went to waste. He pushed past Jalen, sticking his butt out at the two coaches' sons and patting it. "Hey, meatheads. Put your lips right here and kiss this. You see my man on the *news* last night, amigos? Jalen, maybe these two should come to the grand opening tonight and meet all the *Yankees players*?"

Daniel stopped patting his rump and stood up. "Oh, I forgot. No *meatheads* allowed. Come on, Jalen."

"Whatever," Chris spewed. "Calamari makes me puke."

"And the Yankees stink," Dirk added, sputtering.

Daniel stiffened, ready for a fight.

8

JALEN TUGGED HIS FRIEND TOWARD THE BACK OF the bus, knowing that not only would Daniel lose the fight, but that it also would probably get them both kicked off the team. "Thanks, Daniel, but we gotta ignore those two."

"Hot sauce, I don't know about that," Daniel said. "In the dojo they always say 'fight fire with fire.'"

"That's the dojo, amigo." Jalen took a seat second to the back, and Daniel slumped down opposite him. "Those two know nothing about kung fu."

"One day I'm gonna chop that Chris right in the fat part of his neck, and he's gonna go down like an elephant, I swear," Daniel said. "Then he'll know all he needs to know about kung fu."

"Easy, amigo."

"Yeah, you're right." Daniel brightened. "We got a big day, right? 13U? Ninety-foot bases? First time I've pitched in a game from the big mound. You think I'll be okay?"

"Of course you will. It's me I'm worried about. One day of practice, and I looked so bad they were ready to give me my money back."

"You were under a lot of pressure," Daniel said. "Now you're fine."

Outside the window, the sun's first rays glittered through the treetops alongside the highway. Jalen squinted. "I think about everything it took just for me to be here. . . ."

"Yeah, but think about what it all *did*," Daniel said. "Silver Liner is gonna rock, and soon you won't be worried about entry fees or anything."

"I don't know about *anything*."

"Well, most things. I bet you get a phone out of this whole deal," Daniel said.

Jalen looked down the aisle. Nearly every kid on the bus was intent on some kind of screen, either a phone or an iPad. "Yeah, phones aren't so great."

"I don't know. . . ." Daniel looked hungrily at the iPad screen of the kid in front of him. "I saw Cat playing this Plants vs. Zombies game. It looked killer."

"Phones don't help you be a better ballplayer," Jalen said.

"True." Daniel sounded sorry for even hinting at such a thing.

They rumbled along for a few minutes in silence before Daniel spoke again. "Hey, what about doing some of that baseball genius stuff for me?"

Jalen rolled his eyes. "How many different pitches you think you'll see? Guys on this level are just trying to get it over the plate as fast as they can."

Daniel scratched his neck. "Chris throws a curveball."

"Chris," Jalen said with disgust. "How many boy ogres you think we'll see? He's a freak."

"I don't know, Jalen. It's not the Rockton Little League. This isn't even a big tournament, but I think you're gonna see guys like Chris, maybe even better."

"Okay, but would it really help you if you knew the pitch?" Jalen asked.

Daniel shrugged. "Maybe."

"And what if Coach Gamble sees me signaling to you? How's that gonna go over? You think a guy like him is going to be okay with a kid like me coaching his own team around him? I don't."

Daniel peered down the long bus aisle. The back of Coach Gamble's giant head squeezed out from beneath his hatband. He was barking at Coach Benning in the opposite seat, something they couldn't hear. Jalen almost laughed.

The guy was salty even to his own assistant coach.

"Okay, well, it was just an idea." Daniel folded his arms and tugged his hat down like he was taking a nap.

It was a short ride to White Plains, and the team unloaded and got checked in. A festive mood filled the air. There were balloons and banners, uniforms and hats of different colors for the various teams. Crazed parents sipped coffee and whispered among themselves as they evaluated the competition for their own kids. Already a concession trailer churned out the smell of cotton candy, and Jalen automatically scanned the skyline for a Ferris wheel that, of course, wasn't there.

The Rockets' first game, against the team from Sleepy Hollow, was scheduled to start at eight o'clock.

Jalen stayed in the back of the group of players crowding around Coach Gamble as he read off the lineup card. He remained hopeful until the bitter end. After Tuesday's performance, he had to assume he'd bat last if he batted at all, and the final player named was Pauly. Jalen's eyes met Daniel's, and Jalen forced a smile and gave his friend a thumbs-up, determined still to be the best teammate he could be.

Daniel was playing left field and batting seventh. He leaned close to Jalen in the dugout before taking the field. "You could still sub in. Maybe Pauly chokes?"

"I'm not rooting against my own team," Jalen said. "I'll get in. Now, go get a big lead so it can happen."

Daniel grinned and loped off.

The sun climbed quickly, heating dirt, grass, and players alike.

Jalen didn't get off the bench after warm-ups, but he kept his spirits up, cheering on his teammates at the plate and in the field. He knew being a good teammate was an important part of the game. It was something James Yager was known for with the Yankees, and Jalen admired just about everything JY did.

They crushed Sleepy Hollow and went directly to an adjacent field to play a tougher foe, Armonk. Jalen held his breath when Coach Gamble read off the lineup but was disappointed again.

As the sun beat down, Jalen stayed sharp and cheered the guys on, even Chris, who played first base, and Dirk, behind the plate in his catcher's gear. Jalen didn't dare ask, but he could only assume the coaches were saving Chris's arm for the championship game. He'd heard rumblings that the team from Bronxville was favored to win the tournament.

When the Rockets entered the sixth inning of the game with a four-run lead over Armonk, Jalen began to feel the excitement of the possibility that he might play. But

Caleb Paquet gave up a single and a double to start the inning. Then Pauly Ross dropped an easy pop fly in right field, and two runs scored. Jalen bit his cheek and forced himself not to look at Coach Gamble's reaction. He heard Coach Benning curse but kept his eyes on the field. The next batter hit a line drive down the first base line, and Chris snagged it the way a frog snaps up a fly.

The next Armonk batter took advantage of Chris's size by drag-bunting a pitch down the first base line. By the time Chris charged and fielded the ball, Armonk had a man safe at first.

Then the next batter punched one through the hole between first and second. Pauly came up on it but flubbed his throw to second, allowing runners on second and third.

This time, Jalen couldn't keep from glancing over at the coaches.

"Get him outta there, Coach," Dirk's dad urged Coach Gamble.

"Who should I put in?" Coach Gamble looked down at the row of boys on the bench.

The coach caught Jalen's eye. Jalen told himself to be bold. Good things happened to people who were bold.

He nodded confidently and tried to hold the coach's gaze.

Coach Gamble simply looked past Jalen at Sam Watts

and called for him to get his glove and be ready to replace Pauly. Caleb Paquet was still on the mound for the Rockets, and the two runs off Pauly's error seemed to have spooked him. He walked the next batter, filling the bases.

"You gotta pull him, too." Coach Benning spoke like it was just the two coaches and the other kids weren't even there.

"I gotta save Chris. We're gonna need him."

"We won't need him or anyone if you let this circus act go on," replied Coach Benning.

That was when Coach Gamble called time-out.

"Sam, you take first." Coach Gamble spoke into the dugout before heading to the mound as he waved Pauly in. Coach Gamble sent Caleb Paquet to right field before pointing in the direction of Chris and hooking his finger.

Chris looked like a boy with a BB gun in a world full of empty bottles. He warmed up with just three throws before nodding to his dad, then the ump. Jalen made room for Pauly, but his crestfallen teammate kept going past him to the corner of the dugout, where he kicked his own bat.

"Let's go, Chris!" Jalen shouted. "You got this!"

The other boys in the dugout followed Jalen's lead, and soon they were cheering as Chris tore through his first batter with three red-hot strikes.

"You see that?!" Coach Benning slapped Chris's dad a high five. "You *see* that?"

The next batter swung and nubbed a curve into the dirt two feet from home plate. Dirk pounced, scooped it up, and casually stepped back on home plate for the force out. With four pitches, Chris had extracted them from disaster. Although he'd never show it, Jalen couldn't help feeling envious as the enormous sixth grader accepted back slaps from all around and jogged to the dugout.

Armonk was determined to keep Rockton from scoring again and changed to a short, muscular pitcher with a live arm. He sat three Rockets down in order, and Coach Gamble seemed to have no other choice but to rely on Chris to close out the win. If Coach Gamble did plan to get Jalen some action, he certainly forgot in the tension of the other team's rally. Jalen sat the bench for the final inning but cheered anyway when Chris ended it with just six pitches.

As the coaches slapped another high five, Jalen overheard Coach Benning say, "Made it to the championship *and* you saved his arm."

"Dirk looked good too," Coach Gamble said. "That was a major-league play getting his mask off and jumping on that dribbler. We'll need everything we've got to beat this next team."

Excited by getting to play Bronxville in the championship,

the Rockets headed for the bus to stow their equipment and pick up lunch before heading to the picnic area beside the ball fields. Jalen, who'd sat the whole game out, stole a sideways glace at Pauly. He'd nearly lost the game single-handedly, but at least he'd played. Neither looked surprised when Coach Gamble said, "Pauly, DeLuca, you two bring the cooler."

Jalen looked at his father's beat-up blue cooler, but Pauly reached for an enormous gray one, and Jalen helped him lug it to the picnic tables beneath some big shade trees. They hoisted the cooler up on a bench. Jalen caught his breath and looked back at the bus, which Coach Gamble had buttoned up tight.

Jalen hesitated, then swallowed and said, "Coach, I can get my dad's sandwiches. . . ."

Coach Gamble squinted at Jalen, then looked over at the bus and sighed. "I think we're good, but okay. Yup."

The coach dangled some keys in front of Coach Benning. "Go unlock the bus, will you, Coach? You can leave it unlocked, too. I think I want the kids to get off their feet in the AC after lunch."

Coach Benning already had a Subway unwrapped and halfway to his mouth. He frowned and set the sub down before jingling the keys and heading back to the bus. Jalen hurried behind and lifted the cooler out of the bus.

He struggled behind Coach Benning and set his cooler down beside the big one. Everyone already had a sub. Only a few of his teammates even looked, but still Jalen held up a Silver Liner hero. Its aluminum wrapper glinted in the sun. "Grilled marinated chicken with red peppers and provolone," Jalen said. "Anybody want one?"

There was an uncomfortable silence. Coach Gamble grunted, "No," with his mouth full, and Coach Benning shook his head.

Only Daniel sprang forward. "Awesome, amigo. Just what I need after that win."

Jalen and Daniel retreated silently with their food and drinks to a table on the outskirts of the team, sitting by themselves and hardly enjoying the excellent sandwiches.

"Those jerks don't know what they're missing," Daniel complained, his anger rising. "I could have gone in and pitched." He thumbed his chest and looked up with a fire in his dark brown eyes.

Jalen took a swig from his can of iced tea and willed Daniel to relax.

They talked quietly, with Jalen trying to lift Daniel's spirits. By the time they'd balled up their aluminum wrappers and tapped the last drops of tea from their cans, most of the team and the coaches were wandering toward the bus. Jalen saw Pauly and Coach Benning carrying the empty

Subway sandwich cooler between them, and he wondered if he was in trouble for not finishing the job with Pauly when a hoot and a burst of laughter caught his attention.

Back at the center picnic table, Chris and Dirk were flipping aluminum-wrapped sandwiches Frisbee-style at a metal garbage drum. Jalen's mouth fell open as he watched Dirk miss wide left, then Chris drop one in the center with another hoot.

"Hey, that's . . ." Jalen bolted toward them, his chest burning with a white-hot core of rage.

Dirk scored a bull's-eye, and Chris spun a third sandwich into the trash before Jalen arrived and slapped the next one out of his hand on the backswing.

"Ow!" Chris bellowed, and turned to look at Jalen with complete disbelief. "You hit my *arm. My arm!*"

By the tone of his voice, anyone listening might have expected Chris's arm to fall off in a spurt of blood. Jalen took a step back, wondering if he'd somehow destroyed Chris's entire baseball career, as the gigantic bully lowered his head and charged him with an earsplitting roar.

9

STUNNED BY CHRIS'S SUDDEN INSANE REACTION,
Jalen took the other boy's fully loaded shoulder into his
unprotected midsection. His feet left the ground, and he
seemed to float for a moment before crashing into a picnic table. Flares of pain went off in his back and head. His
breath was nowhere to be found, even though he really
wanted to breathe. He somehow ended up in the grass
with Chris planted on top of him, one hand gripping the
front of Jalen's uniform and the other balled up into a fist,
ready to smash Jalen's face.

Jalen saw it coming and winced.

Instead of the snap of breaking bone and cartilage,
Jalen heard the sharp blast of a whistle.

"Chris!!"

Jalen opened his eyes and looked beyond Chris. First he saw Daniel at a standoff with Dirk. Dirk had his fists up, and Daniel stood frozen on one leg in his flying-crane stance. Behind them he saw Coach Gamble, whistle in hand, charging toward them, red-faced and screaming his son's name.

"Stop!" Coach Gamble was like a powerful blast of cold air. Dirk and Daniel dropped their poses. Chris went limp. Jalen let his head fall back into the grass.

Coach Gamble grabbed his son by the scruff of the neck and yanked him off Jalen. He brought his face so close to Chris that their noses nearly touched. "Do you want to hurt your hand and end the season? Do you?"

"No," Chris whined.

"No." His dad released him roughly.

Jalen sat up, feeling scolded even though the coach was ignoring him entirely. Then came the question.

"Now, what happened?" Coach Gamble wasn't asking Jalen. It was as if Jalen didn't exist.

"Dirk and me were cleaning up," Chris said, still whining. "Then this butt-head punched my arm while I was tossing some garbage in the can. He hit me on my back-swing, and I think I tweaked it. . . ."

Coach Gamble tilted his head and glanced at Jalen.

Jalen rubbed the back of his skull, feeling the soreness.

"You *tweaked* it?" Coach Gamble scraped his bottom lip with his teeth. When he looked back at Jalen, it seemed he was about to explode.

Jalen closed his eyes, expecting that his career with travel team baseball was about to end.

10

"JALEN, YOU SAY YOU HIT CHRIS'S ARM TO KEEP him from trashing those sandwiches?"

"My father made those." Jalen swallowed. "He had no right."

"No, he didn't," Coach Gamble said, surprising everyone.

"Huh?" Daniel said, looking as confused as Jalen felt.

The coach grabbed Chris by the collar again. "You don't waste food! This bad attitude has to stop. This morning—shouting at your mother. Refusing to make your bed. Trashing food . . . Hurt your arm? I'll hurt your arm, you do something stupid like that again. . . . And toughen up anyway."

He let Chris loose.

"But Dad . . ." Chris grabbed his elbow, cringing.

"No. Stop that!" Chris's dad clenched his hands by his sides and wobbled his head as he mocked his son. "'I tweaked it. Boo-hoo.' You better get it together by game time."

The coach turned to Jalen and Daniel. The fumes of anger still lingered, and his voice was gruff. "Okay, you guys get this cooler back on the bus, and let's go get warmed up for the big one."

They watched their coach lumber off, shaking his head. "Sandwiches! I've seen it all now."

"Wow," said Daniel. "I thought he was gonna go nuts. Since when can the Prince of Darkness be wrong?"

"Maybe the father's not as bad as the spawn after all."

Daniel watched for another moment with a look of doubt. "Maybe. Come on, let's get these things stowed. You gotta get loose if you're gonna see some action."

"What makes you think I'm seeing action?" Jalen couldn't help feeling a bit excited.

Daniel picked up his side of the cooler. "I don't know. Coach was on your side back there. . . . You haven't played. I just figured . . ."

"Well, I hope you're right."

They stowed the sandwiches, and Coach Benning closed the cargo doors.

There were only thirty minutes before the championship game was scheduled to begin.

Jalen hurried to get on first so he could get to the back of the bus without another confrontation with Chris. He felt a little ashamed but reminded himself he needed to do everything he could to get a chance to play. He and Daniel had decided at lunch that "doing everything" meant that Jalen needed to *ask* Coach Gamble for some playing time.

When they got off the bus and filed into the dugout for the championship game, Jalen made his move. For all he knew, the coach might have simply forgotten about playing him. *As if,* he thought.

Daniel, who'd been all in favor of the move, quickly disappeared as Jalen marched right up to Coach Gamble in the dugout and tapped his shoulder blade.

The big, thick coach turned with a look of disbelief. "Yeah?"

"Coach, I haven't gotten in for even half an inning," Jalen said. "I gotta get in, Coach. Will you let me?"

He tried not to whimper or whine, but he felt his words came out like a teakettle taken off the flame.

"I *gotta* get you in, DeLuca? Gotta?" He snorted. "I highly doubt it."

"But Coach, I think I can do better than Pauly."

"My grandmother could do better than Pauly, and she's

dead." Coach Gamble looked around like he was wanting some backup from Coach Benning. "Look, DeLuca, we talked to you about all this. I warned you about very limited play time, and you wanted to go ahead anyway. You made your own bed here. You did not look good on Tuesday and—heck—you missed Thursday's practice altogether."

"But Coach, I had to help JY on Thursday."

"Help?" Coach Gamble scoffed. "All you did was sit in the stands eating hot dogs and Cracker Jacks. There's no such thing as luck, DeLuca. Even if there was, you gotta make up your mind if you want to be a baseball player or someone's magic rabbit's foot."

His barb hit the mark because it was true. Jalen let his eyes drop to his feet, and he spoke quietly. "I know."

Defeated, he turned to go when Coach Gamble said, "Wait."

11

"LOOK, DELUCA," THE COACH SAID. "I DON'T WANT
you thinking you're not playing because of what happened
with Chris and the sandwiches. I meant what I said. He
was wrong, and I also like your enthusiasm, the way you
cheer the team on. That's commendable. In fact, tell you
what I'll do. . . . If it's a blowout, I'll try to get you in for an
at bat and maybe an inning or two in the field. That's *if*,
though. No promises, okay?"

Jalen grinned. "Okay, Coach. Thanks."

"I said 'if.'"

"I know, Coach."

12

JALEN'S EXCITEMENT WAS SOON PUT TO BED.

The reason the Bronxville Bandits were favored to win became obvious immediately. Their star pitcher, Grady Gertz, was actually better than Chris. He was taller than Chris, if not as big, and could not only throw a curveball and the hottest four-seam fastball Jalen had ever seen from a kid, he also had a changeup that was impossible for the Rockets batters to adjust to after the fastball.

But if Chris was upset about the dressing-down his dad had given him, he didn't let it show. On the pitcher's mound he was all focus, and he avoided Jalen in the dugout, probably to cure himself of the temptation to taunt him.

The pitching duel raged on between Chris and Grady,

and the first four innings ended scoreless, with only three total hits for both teams.

Jalen cheered hard, even though the disappointment of not playing began to worm its way into his heart. He couldn't help remembering the excitement of last night, helping JY and the Yankees win a big game, and it made things even harder today. Still, he cupped his hands around his mouth and shouted, "That's it, Chris. Get another one!"

Just then the Bronxville batter smacked one of Chris's fastballs out of the park. It was the bottom of the fifth inning, and Jalen, like the rest of his team, fell silent. Chris rubbed the elbow Jalen had smacked, and Jalen glanced at Coach Gamble, who frowned. Chris didn't stop, though. He gritted his teeth and reloaded.

The next batter hit a double on the first pitch. The next one had a 1–1 count when he banged it over the fence as well. Three more hits followed, loading the bases before Gertz himself got up and hammered a grand slam home run, making it suddenly a 7–0 blowout.

Coach Gamble called time-out and walked to the mound, where he and Chris argued about him coming out of the game. Coach Gamble said something sharp and walked away, signaling to the umpire and leaving his son to his own fate. Jalen was relieved that Chris left his elbow alone, and even he had to admire the way Chris hung in there to finish the inning, finally getting his third out on a big fly that would have gone over the fence too but for a spectacular leaping catch by Daniel in left field. With one inning to go, the score stood at 7–0.

As he stomped through the dugout, Chris stopped in front of Jalen and pointed at his arm. "You did this. Thanks." He moved on before Jalen could reply.

Jalen opened his mouth to protest, but the looks he got from his other teammates told him he would find no sympathy.

The first two batters up were Dirk and Chris. Whatever went wrong with Chris, the same couldn't be said for Gertz. He sat both the Rockets' best bats down with just eight pitches. When Chris whiffed on three in a row, he slammed his bat into the dirt and cursed the whole way back to the dugout. Jalen averted his eyes and was unpleasantly surprised when Coach Gamble called his name.

"DeLuca!"

"Yeah, Coach?"

"You're up."

"I—" Jalen bounced to his feet, pointing at his own chest. "Me?"

"I said if it was a blowout. This isn't what I was thinking, but I'd have to say it qualifies." Coach Gamble didn't look one bit happy, and Jalen wondered for an instant if batting against Gertz at this point in the game was more of a punishment than a reward for being a good cheerleader.

Either way, he didn't care. Jalen grabbed his bat off the rack, slipped on his gloves, and plunked a helmet down on his head.

"Let's go!" Coach Gamble barked. "I'd like to end the misery sometime this year."

Jalen hurried through the dugout.

When Chris stuck his foot out, Jalen tripped and went down.

Laughter rang out, but Jalen popped up. Without looking back, he dusted off his face and uniform as he marched toward home plate. When he stepped up to the plate, Gertz looked at him and fought back a smile, the sign of a dominant player not wanting to gloat.

Jalen tapped the plate with his bat, took a couple of swings, and hunkered down into his stance. Gertz leaned forward, studying Jalen. He narrowed his eyes, then laughed. "Hey, you're that kid with the Yankees, aren't you?"

The pitcher looked over at the dugout toward his coach and pointed at Jalen. "Coach, it's the Calamari Kid!"

13

JALEN FELT HIS CHEEKS FLUSH WITH EMBAR-
rassment and a touch of pride.

The chatter from the Bronxville players subsided.

"Get him, Grady!" the first baseman shouted.

Grady wiped the smile off his face and brought his glove
to his chest, covering the ball in his other hand. His face
lost all expression, and he went into his windup. The ball
came at Jalen in a blur. He swung so hard his legs cork-
screwed, and he stumbled forward.

The Bronxville players roared with laughter, and the
same delighted sound spilled from the dugout of Jalen's
own team . . . guys he'd cheered on all day.

Jalen clenched his teeth and reminded himself that

both Dirk and Chris had whiffed against Gertz. There'd be no shame in striking out, but looking at Grady, Jalen knew he was going to get a fastball. He took a practice swing and stepped back up to the plate.

Gertz was all business. He wound up and in it came, a smoking pitch right down the center. Jalen shifted his weight and swung fast, this time only trying to connect instead of crushing it.

He missed, but not entirely. The nicked ball flew over the backstop, and at least no one was laughing. Gertz frowned.

"Okay, Grady, end this thing!" shouted the shortstop. "End it right now! You got this guy!"

Gertz took a deep breath and cracked his neck.

That was when Jalen knew exactly what Gertz was going to do, and it wasn't another fastball.

The Bronxville pitcher was going to throw a changeup. Jalen just knew it.

Gertz went into his windup, using the same speed, the same motion as he'd used for the fastball. In the instant before the ball was released, doubt flashed in Jalen's mind, because there was no difference in the delivery of either pitch.

He knew it, though, in that instant, knew the ball would hang out there like an apple on a low branch, and he pushed aside uncertainty—whether or not anyone might laugh. They'd already laughed, treated him like a joke. What did he care if they did it again? But if he *crushed* it? What would they say then?

All that went through his mind in a nanosecond as the pitch came at him.

Jalen swung for the fences.

14

JALEN JOGGED AROUND THE BASES WITHOUT
hearing cheers or the clapping hands of his teammates.
There was only the huff of his own breath and the slight
whistle of air through the earholes of his helmet. His foot
hit the rubber of home plate with a final slap.

"Caleb, you're up. Let's go." Coach Gamble sounded just
as gruff as always. "Nice hit, DeLuca."

Jalen fought back a grin and plunked himself down
on the bench like nothing had happened. His teammates
stopped packing their equipment bags and took their
seats. Daniel snuck up behind Jalen and whispered with
delight, "Amigo! You *crushed* it!"

Caleb went to the plate and promptly struck out.

"Okay, that's it," growled Coach Gamble, heading out of the dugout. "Let's shake hands."

Jalen fell into the back of the line and answered the grinning Bronxville faces with a somber stare. Hitting a home run—he knew—was no excuse for joy when your team got spanked. The Bronxville coaches came last, and after shaking the assistant coach's hand, Jalen was surprised when the head coach took his hand without letting go. The coach steered Jalen a few steps toward the pitcher's mound.

"Hey, you're Jalen DeLuca, right? The kid with the Yankees?"

"Yes," said Jalen, stunned.

"That was some hit," the coach said.

Jalen wanted to tell the coach that it was easy, because he *knew* it was a changeup and that the ball was going to just hang out there for him to smack, but he stopped himself. "Oh. Thanks."

"Yeah." The coach leaned in. "So, I'm wondering why you didn't play? I watched you guys in the first game, and you didn't play then, either. Are you in trouble or something?"

"No."

"Well, your bat looks pretty healthy." The coach chuckled. "Do you struggle in the field?"

"No, I'm not bad." Jalen glanced nervously at his own coaches, but no one on his team, not even Daniel, was paying any attention. "I had a bad practice this week."

"Look, take this." The coach slipped a business card into Jalen's hand. "We could use a bat like yours. You don't see many kids putting one out on Grady. And I know it wasn't just luck. You brought your bat around on his fastball on that second pitch like a pro, nearly got it. Call me if you feel like switching teams. I'm serious. We could use you, and I can promise you this: I wouldn't have you warming the bench."

"Thanks, Coach," Jalen said, hardly believing his luck.

"Coach Allen." The coach grabbed his hand again and tightened his grip before letting go. He seemed sincere, like a man who could be trusted. "I hope I'll hear from you, Jalen. I hate to see talent like yours go to waste."

Jalen couldn't keep from smiling as the two teams lined up and received their awards from the tournament officials. Bronxville players got individual trophies, while the Rockton Rockets got silver medals strung on red ribbons. Jalen felt dazed as he walked toward his own dugout, not worried in the least that he'd missed the first few words of Coach Gamble's rant. When it was over, Jalen couldn't even say for sure what his coach had said other than a few words like "pathetic" and "disgraceful" and that there was a chance they could avenge themselves, since both teams were playing in an even bigger tournament in Boston next weekend.

On board the bus, Jalen joined the rest of the team in depositing his medal into the garbage bag Coach Benning held open as they filed by onto the bus. Coach Gamble had declared that second place was trash, and that's where their medals belonged. Jalen scooted past the head coach's seat and stayed alert for Chris sticking his foot out into the aisle, but the big beefy pitcher seemed too glum to bother with any bullying. In the back of the bus, Jalen sat down directly across the aisle from Daniel.

Daniel sighed. "My mom would have loved that medal. Anything like that in my place goes over big."

"Yeah, well, look at this." Jalen leaned over and showed his friend the card. "That coach asked me if I wanted to play for Bronxville." He kept his voice low, but it trembled with excitement. "He said I wouldn't sit the bench with *them*."

"That is so cool!" Daniel looked at the card, flipping it over. "He put his cell phone on the back, amigo. It's like recruiting, right? I heard of that happening. What you gonna do? I mean, can I go too? You can't leave me here by myself, right?"

Jalen felt the thrill suddenly drain out of him. He hadn't thought of Daniel, but of course he couldn't go without him.

"Well," Jalen said. "I'll call him and ask."

15

DANIEL'S FATHER PICKED THEM UP FROM THE
school parking lot. It was just past six o'clock when they
bumped over the train tracks and Jalen hopped out of the
battered pickup truck in front of the Silver Liner. Jalen
hoisted his dad's cooler from the backseat.

"So, you gonna call that coach?" Daniel asked.

"Tomorrow," Jalen said. "I don't want to seem desperate. Okay?"

"Sure." Daniel grinned.

"See you in a little bit," he said, before slamming the
car door.

Jalen stood for a moment outside his father's restaurant, its lights already ablaze in the evening light. It

was miraculous to him, but in the world of James Yager, miracles seemed commonplace. Only a few days ago, the diner had its windows smashed in by firemen and the kitchen was a blackened hole. Now it looked brand-new, as if the shiny silver dining car that made up the front section of the restaurant had just been pulled from the railroad tracks. Inside, every employee his dad had ever hired seemed to be buzzing about, setting up for the first seating, which kicked off at six thirty. There were three seatings after that, at seven thirty, eight thirty, and nine thirty. Guests would be served family-style from a fixed menu so the Silver Liner could turn over the tables fast, serving several hundred diners the now-famous food.

Jalen found his dad in the sparkling kitchen, busy as a circus juggler. Fragrant steam rose from multiple pots and pans along the giant stovetop. He set the cooler down on an empty shelf.

"You're here!" His father wiped his hands on a messy white apron and hugged Jalen, kissing his cheeks. "Look! Look! Is all ready. Everyone giving me things, the drinks, the fish. . . . Everyone knows about Mr. JY, and they wanna be a part of this. It's gonna be an opening like no one ever before. I got fifty pounds of the calamari. They gonna love it!"

"Dad, can I help?"

"No, no, no. I got plenty of people. You go change.

Mr. Yager gonna be here for the seven thirty seating. Hey!" His father arched his back and eyed Jalen, sensing his mood. "How was you game? Did you get a hit?"

Jalen beamed. "I did. A home run off the best pitcher in the tournament."

"See? You had the sandwiches, and your team they won the championship, and my boy he's hitting the home run!" Jalen's dad nodded toward the cooler and threw his hands in the air.

"Well, we lost in the championship," Jalen said.

"So, runners-up. Second place, she's a good thing. Like a silver medal for the Silver Liner. Is also good luck. Everything she's happening good. You go. Get a shower an' come right back so you can be the one to greet Mr. James Yager."

Jalen hadn't seen his dad this happy in quite some time, and he turned that over in his mind as he crunched down the gravel drive that looped around a wetland area before coming to their house by the tracks.

Inside, he showered quickly. He *did* want to be the one to greet JY. There would likely be some TV cameras there, and he'd love nothing more than to upset Chris and Dirk by appearing on the flat-screens inside their homes. That notion caused him to whistle to himself as he dressed. He pulled the nicest short-sleeved collar shirt he owned over his head, and the whistle faded. His eyes had fallen on the picture of his mother, and he realized that with all the tension and excitement of the day, he hadn't thought about her once.

He picked up the framed photo and sat down on the edge of his bed, studying her face, wondering. Where was she? Who was she? Would she want to see him? Was she even alive? He returned the picture to its spot and set off for the diner. Along the way he thought about finding her. Cat was talking about him getting paid by JY to predict pitches. He could use that money to pay a detective, but he felt the best chance was for her to hear about him, the wonder kid, the baseball genius. Then she'd call, wanting to meet him.

He was excited just to be seen in the background with JY, the lucky rabbit's foot, the Calamari Kid. But what if *he* was the story? What if people knew he wasn't just some trinket JY liked to keep close, but a baseball genius? What kind of story would that make? He'd be on *SportsCenter* for sure. And why wouldn't they want him on *Good Morning America* or the *Today* show? And magazines like *Sports Illustrated* or *ESPN?* Maybe even *People* or the *New York Times.* CNN would surely do a story, and so might the big network news shows.

In his mind, all those possibilities led to one thing: his

mom might see him, hear his name, and then just reach out. She would realize that he was a good kid, polite, humble, smart—no, not just smart, a *genius*, at least when it came to baseball. Possibly she'd regret having left Jalen, missing all those childhood years, but she might want to be part of all the exciting things to come.

He rounded the bend and saw the TV trucks, two of them with lights set up and cameras ready, in front of the steps to the diner. The parking lot was full, but more cars continued to arrive and were now filling up the train station's spaces. Jalen saw—and heard—JY's Ferrari coming, and he hurried toward the diner. The Ferrari crawled into the lot, and Jalen moved the orange cone holding a spot so JY could park right in front. Jalen hustled as a handful of reporters and a group of fans converged on the car.

JY got out and looked around, ignoring everyone until he spotted Jalen in the back. JY beamed at him and parted the crowd. "Hey! It's the Calamari Kid!"

JY clasped Jalen's hand and pulled him into a manly hug before turning back to the cameras. Holding Jalen's hand high in the air, he declared, "Here he is, my lucky charm!"

The reporters began to shout over one another. Fans waved photos, caps, and gloves for JY to sign.

"How much money are they offering?"

"Sign my glove!"

"How many games do you plan on batting a thousand?"

"Can you sign my card?"

"Do you have any hard feelings toward Jeffrey Foxx for even suggesting the end of your career was at hand?"

JY held up his hands and said, "No autographs tonight, please. If I do one, I'll have to do a hundred, and we're here to celebrate Fabio's Silver Liner reopening. I'm happy to do some selfies inside after we eat, but I want to get in there because that stuffed calamari is waiting for me, and we go on the road to Cleveland tomorrow. The team and my agent are negotiating as we speak. All good there, no hard feelings. And batting a thousand? I expect to bat a thousand every game from here on out. Ha-ha! At least that's my goal. Now come on inside!"

JY put an arm around Jalen and swept him up the steps and into the diner. The dining car was jammed with people standing with drinks or sitting at the counter while they waited for a table of their own or ordered appetizers and gawked at the patrons in the larger dining room off to the side of the old railcar. Greta—his father's main waitress—had dressed for the occasion and was serving as a hostess. She batted her ridiculously long fake eyelashes at JY as she guided them through the six-thirty diners to a section roped off in the back corner. Cat and her mom were already there, sitting at a big round table.

The crowd was festive, and waitresses with steaming plates of calamari weaved in and out through the tables. In the background, Jalen's dad's favorite music—Andrea Bocelli's singing—could be heard through the sound system. Jalen swelled with importance as he sat down next to JY. He wanted to discuss business, but with the noise and the excitement, it didn't seem to be the right time or place.

Soon Masahiro Tanaka and Brett Gardner arrived, then CC Sabathia with his wife, and finally Daniel arrived and sat down next to Jalen, rounding out their table. A waitress brought drinks and a large platter of stuffed calamari swimming in red sauce, along with pasta and chicken dishes guests could eat family-style. JY led the way, serving Cat and her mom before filling his own plate.

Greta appeared, flushed with excitement. "Mr. Yager, the TV people want to know if they can bring their cameras in to get some shots."

JY stood up. "Of course. Jalen, go get your dad, will you?"

Jalen slipped through the tables and into the kitchen. It surprised him to see his father not busy, but sitting in his office talking to a man in jeans and a dress shirt. The man had his phone out and was holding it like he was recording Jalen's dad.

"Dad? Is everything okay?"

"Jalen!" His father sprang out of his seat and steered Jalen away from the office door. "What do you need?"

"Well, JY wants you out there for the TV people." Jalen tried to see past his dad into the office. "Dad, who is that?"

His father sighed deeply and shook his head, obviously mystified. "Jalen, you not gonna believe this."

Jalen's heart froze. "Well, tell me."

16

JALEN'S FATHER GLANCED OVER HIS SHOULDER toward the office. "That man in there, Jalen . . . he's from the *New York Times*. He had the early dinner—I didn't even know he was here—an' he's gonna do a restaurant review on *Fabio's Silver Liner*."

"Is it bad?" Jalen asked because of the look on his father's face. "The review?"

His father's eyebrows jumped over the rims of his small round glasses. "Bad? No, it's not bad. It's good! He loves my *nonna*'s food! That's why I gotta finish talking to him, but I don't wanna say no to Mr. JY an' the TV, either."

"Dad, just tell the *New York Times* guy. He'll understand.

He'll wait. It'll be a good part of the story that JY wants to help you and have you on TV."

"But this is the thing," Jalen's dad whispered proudly. "This man, he's not caring about JY and the Yankees players. He's loving the *food*. It's my dream come true, Jalen. The *New York Times*!"

"Well, let's just ask him. Is he nice?"

"Yes!"

"Then he'll be fine. Come on."

Still, his dad was nervous, twisting his apron into a knot as he asked the reporter if he could wait just a few minutes while he did some TV with JY.

The reporter laughed easily. "Of course. I'll wait right here, Fabio. Do the TV. They're a lot less patient than us writers."

Back in the restaurant, JY put an arm around Jalen and his dad as the cameramen began to record. Several reporters held out their microphones.

"This is the guy who does it all." JY patted Fabio on the back. "Fabio makes the best Italian food I've ever had and—strange as it may sound—it's this stuffed calamari he's serving everyone tonight that's responsible for getting me out of my slump."

Jalen's dad's cheeks burned from the attention, but he cleared his throat and spoke in a strong voice. "I wanna welcome everyone to my place. This is my dream, to have the big restaurant that everybody wants to come and eat the food my *nonna* teach me how to cook back in Italy. Mr. JY, I thank you and all you teammates for coming tonight, and most of all I thank you for having the Silver Liner rebuilt in just a few days after the fire. You're an angel to me an' my boy."

The two men shook hands, and JY took a selfie with Fabio on his phone before tweeting it out to his three-million-plus followers. Jalen's dad returned to his office in the kitchen while the TV cameras shot some more video of JY and his teammates eating and joking with one another about the Cleveland pitching staff. In the midst of all the food and talking and laughter, Jalen found himself staring at the cameras and their small red lights.

He felt a jab in his ribs and realized that Cat had swapped seats with JY so he could sit next to her mom. "Ouch!"

"I asked you twice if you ever get tired of eating cephalopods." Cat held up a white ring of squid on the end of her fork.

"You don't like cephalopods?" Jalen joked, figuring her fancy word was what squids were called in science books. "You gotta get Dad's stuffing with it and some sauce. I don't eat just the fish part."

"Well, I always like to take things down to their basic elements and see what's going on beneath the surface, so . . ." She let the white ring drop into the sauce on her plate, mixed it around, and scooped it up with some stuffing before shoveling it into her mouth.

"I never get tired of it because we don't eat it that much," Jalen said. "That stuffing is filled with crabmeat. It's expensive."

"You won't have to worry about that after tonight." Cat looked around at the crowd. "This place is a gold mine."

"Now it is, thanks to you."

"I wasn't fishing for compliments." Cat took a sip of sparkling water. "Or cephalopods. Ha—get it, fishing?"

"I know, but the whole thing about JY tweeting and the lucky calamari," Jalen said. "Even fixing up the diner after the fire . . . it was all you."

"Only I can't tell you what the next pitch is gonna be, so I guess we're a good team." Cat held out her fist, and Jalen bumped it.

Jalen leaned close so no one except Cat would hear. "I still feel bad about saying that stuff about JY and your mom being an item."

"Well . . . ," she said, angling her head over her shoulder to glance at her mom and JY laughing together, "Look, JY is awesome, and there's really no love lost between me and my stepfather, but I hate to see her make things all complicated again."

"You wouldn't have to move very far," Jalen said, kidding because JY's mansion was just the other side of a big stone wall surrounding Cat's stepfather's estate.

"I don't know if they're going to end up together," she said. "I don't think anything's going on, but I see the way she looks at him and him at her. And, if she does make a change, we have no idea how long JY will be in Rockton. That wasn't a glowing reception he got from Foxx after the game. I'd say JY's chances are fifty-fifty to stay with the Yankees, and I don't know how he can do at the plate without you there calling the pitches."

"Why wouldn't I be there?"

"You're not flying to Cleveland with the Yankees tomorrow, are you?"

Everything had been happening so fast and so intensely that Jalen hadn't thought past the Silver Liner's grand opening. "No, I guess not. We've got school Monday."

"Right," Cat said, "two more days of school. Then the Yankees are home against Houston. Then they go to Boston, then Baltimore. And what about the Rockets? You've got practices and games yourself. I don't want to spoil the night for you, but the whole thing is a mess."

"Then why did you?" Jalen asked.

"Why did I what?" Cat screwed up her face.

Jalen stared at her. "Spoil the night."

"You can't just bury your head in the sand, Jalen. This is real."

"This is the biggest night of my father's life." Jalen waved his hand around at all the people.

"Which is why it'd be a shame to have the whole thing collapse after one big weekend," Cat said.

"Why would it collapse?" Jalen snorted.

"People are fickle," she said. "One minute you're on top of the world, next minute you're yesterday's news. We need JY to keep batting a thousand—if not every game, at least on a regular basis—and we need him to keep tweeting about the diner. *That's* how you create a franchise. It takes a lot more than a big opening night."

Jalen realized she was right. He hadn't wanted to think about the big picture. It was complicated. He couldn't imagine how all the pieces could possibly fit together, and he hadn't even told Cat his plan about finding his mother.

"So, I'm guessing you've got an idea?" Jalen said.

Cat raised an eyebrow. "Don't I always?"

17

JALEN HAD TO WAIT TO HEAR CAT'S PLAN UNTIL
they were back at JY's mansion.

After eating and taking pictures with fans in the dining room, the players all decided to finish the night by shooting some pool in JY's man cave. Jalen was familiar with the large, dark-paneled room and its thick leather furniture. He'd been there on the day he proved to JY that he could really predict the next pitch in an MLB game. They'd watched a live game on the huge flat-screen. Jalen had been awed by all the framed photos of JY and famous people like President Obama, Peyton Manning, and Denzel Washington. JY had been awed by Jalen's baseball genius.

Now they sat together in JY's office, with its shelves

lined with unread books. JY sat behind his desk, bending and unbending a paper clip. Jalen and Cat sat in chairs facing the desk, while Daniel and Cat's mom took the couch. The rest of JY's guests were already downstairs. Cat, however, had insisted on a formal meeting.

"So," Cat said, "we're here to talk about next steps and work out a deal with you and Jalen."

"And you're his agent, right?" JY sighed. "I know you're going to drive a hard bargain. What is it?"

Cat narrowed her eyes, slowly nodding her head, assessing her adversary. "Originally, I was pretty set on ten thousand dollars per game along with a cell phone."

Jalen's mouth dropped. "Ten thou—"

Cat cut him off. "Stop. I'm handling this."

Cat cleared her throat. "Look, I do think it's worth ten, but we're all friends, so I think we can do it for less. Maybe shave a few thousand."

JY looked at Cat's mom. "Is she for real?"

"I'm thinking she is," Cat's mom said. "She's got that look."

"She's twelve years old," JY said. "Don't tell me you can't control her."

Cat's mom shrugged. "I lost control about eight years ago. I fought it at first, but life's too short. Her brother? He'll FaceTime me to help pick which shirt to wear. This one is twelve going on twenty, so I'm just the driver in all this."

"Yeah, the getaway driver. For a bank robbery." JY laughed at his own joke, glanced at Jalen, then directed his attention to Cat. "Ain't gonna happen."

"Under your contract, you take home about eighty thousand a game." Cat seemed unaffected. "You were about to make zero per game next year, until Jalen came along."

"And I helped him." JY pointed at Jalen but kept his eyes on Cat as he counted off on his fingers. "I didn't press charges for breaking into my batting cage and stealing those baseballs. I paid his travel team fee. I talked his coach into letting him miss practice, and I've turned his dad's place into a tourist attraction. That's *after* I had a contractor practically rebuild the place in four days."

"Yes," Cat said, "that was fine to get this kicked off, but now we're talking about moving forward. Jalen can change your *career*. He could change the destiny of an entire team."

"What team?" JY blinked. "What are you talking about now?"

Cat tilted her head. "Well, it's a marketable skill, predicting pitches. Why couldn't he help an entire team? That'd be worth more than ten thousand a game, that's for sure."

Jalen nodded because that did make sense.

JY frowned. "You heard Jeffrey Foxx. That's just not going to happen. He's not going to admit that anyone can have a bigger impact on winning a title than he does—certainly not a kid like Jalen."

"Who said it has to be the Yankees?" Cat puckered her lips. "Not that that's what we want."

JY looked at Cat's mom again. "Oh yeah, this is great. Just great. Can you *believe* this?"

Cat's mom shook her head and raised her hands helplessly.

JY sat back and huffed, then said, "Okay, listen. I've been thinking. Jalen has his own baseball to play, and he can't travel across the country with me even if he didn't. It's not practical for him to be with me every game, and I'm hoping I won't need him. I was in a slump, but I think I'm out of it now. I don't have to bat a thousand every game, either. That's just not happening, even if I do know every pitch."

Jalen shook his head in disbelief. Was the whole thing over?

"So here's my offer," JY continued. "A couple times a week, five or six times a month, maybe, I use Jalen to keep my average up."

JY looked directly at him now. "I give you five hundred

dollars a game, and I keep eating at your dad's place . . . say once a week with a tweet every other week. That's worth a lot."

Jalen opened his mouth to say yes, but Cat leaned over, grabbed his arm with one hand, and thumped her chest with the other. "I got this."

18

"IF YOU SAY FIVE HUNDRED—WHICH I THINK IS
insulting—then I say nine thousand five hundred," Cat
said.

Jalen dug his fingers into the leather arms of his chair.

"Okay, I see where this is headed." JY snapped the
paper clip in two, smiled, and put his elbows on the desk.
"We go back and forth and end up at five thousand, but
that is not happening. Like I said, I feel like I've got my
groove back anyway. Jalen was a big help, but I helped
him, too, and now we can go our separate ways and part
friends before you or I get upset about this."

"But—" Jalen began to protest.

"No, I get it." JY cut him off, holding his hand out at Jalen like a traffic cop. "Thanks, Cat, but I'm good. I got my groove back. It was a win for everyone, so let's part friends."

"Yeah, I hear you," said Cat, "but it'll change. You'll be back, and I just want you to know the deal. Five hundred is not going to do it. No hard feelings on our side either."

She stood up and extended her hand across the desk. "It's just business."

JY stood up too. He laughed and shook her hand. "Good. I'm glad we're all okay. Now, you guys are all welcome to hang out. We can put on the ball game. I got plenty of sodas. Victoria? Can I get you one?"

"Jalen's ready to fall on his face," Cat said. "Can you take us home, Mom, then come back?"

"Of course I can take you. I'm tired myself."

Jalen began to raise his hand in protest, but he let it drop. "Okay."

Cat was right. He was absolutely exhausted, and the thought of his bed suddenly became irresistible. Aside from that, he sensed Cat wanted to talk to him about her strategy and what she thought would happen next.

At the door, JY shook Jalen's hand. "Thanks, buddy. This was great. Good luck to you and your dad. And I'll try to get in there and have some of that calamari anyway. Maybe tweet about it once in a while too. I don't want you to think I'm sour."

Jalen suddenly felt like crying, but he bit his cheek and said thanks and good-bye and got into the back of the Range Rover. He was cold and empty. Everything had changed in just a few moments. Everything he thought would happen was now ruined, and he was helpless to fix it. The spurt of publicity would end, and without any money for predicting pitches, he wouldn't be able to pay for a detective.

The search for his mother would be impossible.

19

AS THEY DROVE DOWN OLD POST ROAD, JALEN
tapped Cat on the shoulder.

"I wanted to keep helping him," he said.

"Me too," Daniel chimed in.

She turned to them. "I know. You will."

"Cat?" Jalen pleaded with his eyes.

"Unfortunately for our friend, he's going to be right back in his slump, so just relax," she said. "When he gets back from Cleveland, he'll be begging you to get to Yankee Stadium, and then ten grand a game won't seem expensive at all."

"But if he does well, it's over," Jalen said. "I'm finished."

Cat shook her head. "No way does that happen. I'd bet everything I have."

"What do you have?" Cat's mom looked over at her.

"It's just a saying," Cat said. "Like, 'If he bats a thousand, I'll eat my hat.'"

"He's not gonna have to bat a thousand," Daniel said. "Anyone batting above .250 is legit. He's still JY."

"See?" Jalen pointed at Daniel.

"You can't do it for five hundred dollars," Cat said. "That's not fair. He needs to appreciate what you can do, and he will. Just trust me. I can manage him."

"You're managing a future Baseball Hall of Famer?" Daniel raised his eyebrows.

"Who got him to call Coach Gamble?" Cat said. "Who got him to tweet about the Silver Liner? To pay the rest of Jalen's fee?"

"That was all you, Cat," Jalen said.

She lit up with a smile. "That's right. You were gonna do all this in the beginning just to keep him from pressing charges over the baseballs we took. You saw your dad's face tonight. I'm not bragging, but you guys have to trust my instincts."

Jalen sighed and said, "Okay. You're right. I'm sorry. It's just hard to wait without knowing."

"I'm sorry it's that way," she said. "But you know how you can just tell what the next pitch will be?"

"Yeah."

"Maybe I'm a business genius." She shrugged. "I don't know, but I think so."

Jalen smiled and said, "Could be."

But Daniel rolled his eyes. "Right now this whole thing is hot sauce. And if making a mess of things is what it takes to be a genius, then you can call me Einstein."

They pulled up in front of the Silver Liner. The lot was still packed with cars overflowing into the train station.

"Looks like your dad will be busy all night," Cat's mom said. "Want me to drop you home?"

Jalen felt he should go in and help, but he was truly exhausted. "When I told my dad I was going to JY's, he said he'd see me at home, so you can take me if you don't mind."

They drove to his house. Jalen was thankful for the darkness that blanketed the place, but then he wished lights were on and he had his mom there waiting to greet him. As the Range Rover's taillights slipped into the night, the emptiness inside pressed down on him. He made quick work of the bathroom and stripped out of his clothes, leaving a short trail to his bed.

Before putting out the light, he took his mother's

picture off the top of the dresser and brought it back to his bed. He ran his fingernail back and forth over the little metal knobs decorating the frame, and the raspy sound reminded him of the gourd in music class—the guiro, his teacher had called it. He stopped the music and thought of his father, lifted by a balloon of excitement, rising up to the clouds, and his mother, gone long ago, chasing her own dream.

For Jalen's dreams to come true, one of his favorite baseball players of all time was going to have to fall flat on his face over the next four days.

He'd never felt so alone.

20

JALEN WOKE EARLY TO THE SMELL OF ONIONS AND
potatoes frying in the pan.

Rain pattered lightly against the window. He yawned
and stretched, then fished the picture frame out of his
covers and replaced it on the dresser. He pulled on some
sweatpants and a T-shirt, used the bathroom, and wan-
dered into the kitchen. The back of his father's bald head
gleamed even in the gray light falling through the windows. Breakfast snapped and sizzled on the stove.

"Hi, Dad."

His father spun around, spatula in hand. "Jalen! I'm
making you breakfast. You gotta look and see what I got
on the table. We gonna go get phones, you and me."

"What? Phones?" Jalen turned toward the table where they ate. Two places were laid out atop the red-and-white-checkered cloth. Between the settings were three fat bundles of money. "What do you mean, Dad?"

The only phones they'd ever had were the one in the diner and a cheap TracFone they used sparingly.

"That's just the cash!" His father pointed with the spatula, bubbling with delight. "Last night we made almost twelve thousand dollars! That there is just the cash. Most of it was credit cards, but the money we gonna spend today."

Jalen thought of the deal Cat had tried to negotiate with JY. This outdid even that. "But Dad, it's just the opening night. That's not gonna happen all the time."

His father hurried around the counter and picked a black book out from beneath the money stacks. "Look at this. She's my reservation book. Greta, I make her write it down off the computer. I don't trust no computer. Look. The Silver Liner, she's booked full for the next three and a half weeks already! Last week, the bank, she's putting me under the squeeze. I was worried about how I'm gonna keep the diner. Today we gonna get iPhones!"

They were happily planning to go right after breakfast when Jalen suddenly sniffed the air. "Dad, the onions."

"Oh!" His father hurried back to the stove and quickly began flipping things amid a hissing cloud of steam. "It's okay. I got a couple burned, but it's gonna be fine. You sit. I got eggs right here and it's only gonna be three minutes. Have a juice. Have two!"

His father poured the eggs in, crumbled some cheese on top, and gave the whole thing a few mixes and turns before he spun around, beaming. "Jalen! Drink a whole gallon of juice. We are not gonna have to worry about money no more! We are gonna be rich!"

The idea lit a small ember of hope in Jalen's chest. Having a phone, being "rich"—although Jalen knew it wouldn't be rich like JY or Cat's stepfather—would make life a lot easier. He wouldn't have to worry about fees for travel teams or equipment or batting cage time. He wouldn't have to borrow people's phones. He could focus on his game and turn *himself* into a major league player.

He wouldn't need JY to get him into stadiums. He'd be playing there. And his mother? It might take longer, but he could imagine her seeing him stepping up to the plate in the World Series, realizing—as Joe Buck discussed his background—that he was the son she'd left behind.

It was a longer, harder road, but it was still possible.

His dad brought the pan over to the table and served his eggs, onions, potatoes, and cheese out on both their plates. Jalen waited for him to put the pan in the sink and return with a mug of coffee before digging in.

The flavors mixed and exploded in his mouth. "It's amazing."

"Is *nonna*'s recipe." His dad looked at the ceiling. "She's lookin' down on us now and she'd be so happy. . . ."

They polished their plates clean before Jalen's dad said, "I think we gotta get a house. Our own house with a new bathroom and bedrooms up the stairs."

Jalen choked on his juice and had a small coughing fit before he could speak. "A house? Really?"

"Why not?" His dad looked around at the cracked ceiling and walls. His eyes stopped at a jagged hole in a panel board sprouting tufts of pink insulation. "Maybe with a fireplace. I'm always thinking about a nice fire in the winter. And air-conditioning for the summer. That's what we're gonna have."

"Dad, after one night? You sure?"

"Is not just one night, Jalen. When people are reading about us in the *New York Times*, they gonna come from a long way to eat at the Silver Liner, and now with all this money," his father said, picking up a bundle of bills, "everything's gonna be so fresh and so good they gonna come back again and again."

"Yeah," Jalen said, "but Dad, are you sure he's gonna write something that's that good? I mean, people say all the time that you can't trust newspaper reporters."

"I tell you what." His father picked up their plates and utensils and headed for the kitchen as he spoke. "We gonna go find out right now."

"It's in the *Times* today?" Jalen said. "That fast?"

"He said for the Sunday edition—today."

The van's engine struggled, then roared. They stopped at the drugstore in town, and Jalen ran in for the thick stack that was the Sunday *New York Times*. He jumped back in out of the rain and thumped it down on the console between them. His father fished through the sections until he came up with the Metro section. He turned to the last page and jabbed it with a stubby finger. "She's here. . . ."

Jalen struggled to decipher what it said upside down, and instead chose to read the expression on his father's face as he silently mouthed the words.

21

HIS FATHER'S MOUTH STRETCHED INTO A GRIN.

He looked up at Jalen and tapped the paper. "I told you! Listen, Jalen. Listen to what he says: 'Authentic and exquisite! While everyone is looking for the next innovation, Fabio DeLuca has looked back and given us the reason we seek out and adore culinary excellence.' Jalen, they talking about ME!!"

Jalen hugged his father tight, and he thought maybe the slight tremble in his father's frame also brought some tears, but he pretended not to notice and looked away when his father let go and dabbed his face on the hem of his white V-neck T-shirt.

They were at the mall by nine for the opening and got free iPhones for signing up with a carrier's special package. His dad then insisted he buy Jalen some new clothes at TJ Maxx. In short order he had a new pair of jeans, some khaki shorts, polo shirts, and a pair of Docksiders. As soon as they got back into the van, Jalen began to explore some of the things his new phone could do.

"It's got a camera." He snapped a picture of his dad giving him a thumbs-up. "And there's all these apps that don't even cost anything."

Jalen stayed busy with the phone until they arrived at home.

"You do your homework first, then come help me at the diner," his dad said, letting Jalen off before heading for the Silver Liner. "Enough on that phone, okay? We gotta have some rules."

"Okay, Dad," Jalen said, thinking, *Right after two calls.* He flew into the house and dialed up Cat.

"Hello?"

"Guess who?"

"Jalen?"

Jalen laughed. "You were right, the Silver Liner is a gold mine. This is my new phone. You gotta show me how Twitter works and Instagram and all that other stuff. Can you believe it? Me, in the twenty-first century?"

"You were always in the twenty-first century," Cat said. "Not every twelve-year-old kid has a phone."

"I know," he said, "but it sounded good."

"Daniel told me the Rockets have practice later."

"If it stops raining we do."

"He also told me about the Bronxville coach asking you to switch teams. . . ."

Jalen tried to detect any annoyance in Cat's voice. "Yeah, I was gonna tell you. Things have been crazy."

"It sounds good."

"I'd make the change right now," he said, "but I have to make sure Daniel can come too."

"'Cause you need them to drive you?" Cat teased. She knew that Daniel's parents gave Jalen rides to and from practice like clockwork. Their path to Simon Park or just about anywhere went right through town, and Jalen would wait on the corner for a ride.

"Not just that," Jalen said. "Daniel and I have been playing together since second grade, even though you have no idea how much I'd love to get away from Chris and his dad."

Cat went quiet for a moment before she said, "I can't believe he tried to help Jeffrey Foxx by spying on us."

"You never should have trusted him, Cat. He's a big fat jerk."

"My mom always tells me that people can change, and if you don't expect the best, you'll always get the worst."

"Well, you expected the best and got the worst." Jalen remembered the sound of Chris's laughter as he tossed perfectly good sandwiches into the garbage. "Or, maybe that was his best. I don't think he can be anything but a rotten creep."

"Forget about him," Cat said. "Want to come over tonight and watch the Yankees game with me?"

"So we can root against JY like Red Sox fans?" Jalen said. "How crazy will that be?"

"Don't think of it as rooting against him. We'll be rooting *for* you. My mom said we could order pizza."

"I think I can," Jalen said. "I've got to get my homework done—it's just some math and a survey for my shop class, but we get five points for doing it—and then I'm gonna help my dad at the diner until practice. I'm pretty sure he won't mind. All of a sudden, it's not hard for him to get help."

"That happens when you're famous."

"So count me in. Okay, here goes nothing with Bronxville." Jalen hung up and dialed Coach Allen with trembling fingers.

22

"COACH ALLEN? IT'S JALEN DELUCA."

"Hey, Jalen, the Calamari Kid." The coach answered like they were old friends. "I am very glad you called. So, are you with us? We've got a tournament in Boston next weekend. If we get you going by tomorrow, I'll have you ready to play."

Jalen's mouth went dry, and he tried to swallow before he said, "Coach, I was hoping you could take my friend Daniel Bellone, too. He was the kid who made that incredible catch. He's a great pitcher, but that position pretty much belongs to the coach's son. Daniel's not that big, but he's really accurate, so he can nick the low inside corner of the zone. . . ."

Jalen had so much more he wanted to say about his friend, but he realized that Coach Allen had gone quiet.

"Coach?" he asked.

"Yeah, I'm here," said the coach. "Uh . . . look, I've got a full bullpen and—"

"He can play third, too," Jalen added quickly, "really anywhere. He's got a good glove and he's a solid hitter."

"Right . . ." Coach Allen sighed. "Listen Jalen, I really only have one spot. Your guy might have a decent bat and be a serviceable player, but that's not what the Bandits are about. Our guys are all future prospects. If they're not, I don't take them. You . . . well, I see something in you. Like I said, the way you stood up to Gertzy and then popped one over the fence, you'd fit in. But if it's not you, I've got a list of a dozen talented kids who'd love to be on the Bandits. So . . ."

"So it's take it or leave it, huh?" Jalen asked.

"Yeah, I guess it is," said the coach. "Sorry . . ."

Jalen's mind whirred and his stomach flopped. He wavered between thinking Daniel would understand and knowing he wouldn't.

The coach cleared his throat. "Jalen? You there?"

"Yes," Jalen croaked.

"So, what do you think? I'd hate to see you sitting the bench all summer. That can't be good for you. Are you with us, or not?"

23

IT HURT JALEN TO ADMIT IT, BUT WHAT HIS
mother had done to him and his father had tied a
choke knot into some vital heartstring. If the truth was
to be told, she had abandoned them. If the truth was
to be told, he couldn't imagine anyone doing such a
thing. So loyalty was high on Jalen's list of admirable
qualities.

Only something that powerful could make Jalen swallow his hopes and his dreams and say, "No, not without
Daniel. I'm sorry, but I just can't."

In the silence that hung between him and the coach,
Jalen tried to imagine a world where Coach Gamble came
to rely on him. Stranger things had certainly happened.

Sports was the kingdom of fantastic turnarounds, Cinderella stories they were called.

"Okay," Coach Allen finally said. "I tried."

"Thank you, Coach," Jalen replied. "I appreciate the offer."

"Last chance . . ."

Jalen took breath. "No, but thank you."

Coach Allen wished him luck.

Jalen knocked off his homework at the kitchen table. He had two pages of math along with the survey. Even though their teacher had introduced them to trigonometry during the last full week of school, the math was a snap. Jalen got math the way he got baseball. He couldn't explain how he knew, he just knew. There'd been a time when the teachers had made a big fuss about his math knowledge, so much so that it frightened him and he began answering the complex problems they'd given him incorrectly on purpose. He'd been afraid because they started treating him like a freak, pulling him out of his classes and whispering about him. Fitting in was hard enough already.

He finished his schoolwork and listened to the rain patter for a minute. He heard and felt a low, growing rumble before a train rushed past the house with a blaring horn. A framed fishing picture of him and his dad danced in its spot on the shelf, along with three seashells from a day trip to Sherwood Island.

The train's brakes squealed as it slowed to enter the station. There were always fewer trains on the weekends. A beam of sunlight passed by the window, signaling the possible end of the rain. Jalen stepped onto the porch and saw the tattered sky through the bright new leaves above. He found a weather app on his phone. It also promised an end to the rain, and that meant baseball practice with the Rockets would be a go.

"And there's no escaping the Rockets," Jalen said aloud to himself.

He changed into his practice uniform, shouldered his gear bag, and headed toward the diner. His dad had a full crew there, but there was plenty for Jalen to do during lunch. The diner was busy right through the afternoon, with a full reservation book for dinner. Jalen felt bad leaving his dad, but his father wasn't hearing any of that.

"It's a dream come true, Jalen. I love it." His father waved toward the busy stovetop, then wiped his hands on his apron before placing them on Jalen's cheeks. "This isn't work for me. Now, you go and play baseball and then have fun with you friends. I see you tonight. Late!"

Jalen left with the sound of his dad's happy laughter ringing in his ears.

Daniel's dad picked him up in the center of town. Jalen

waited until they'd been dropped off in the parking lot behind the ball field before he showed Daniel his iPhone, because he didn't want Mr. Bellone to feel uncomfortable. One of the things that bonded Jalen and Daniel through the years was being part of only a handful of kids in Rockton whose families *didn't* have a lot of money.

"Nice. Now you can have your own Twitter account, Calamari Kid, or something." Daniel turned the phone over in his hands like a gem, without a trace of envy in his voice, before he handed it back to Jalen. "So, did you call the Bronxville coach?"

"Yeah," Jalen said. "He wasn't as excited about having me . . . us . . . as I thought, so . . ."

Daniel's face fell. He glanced at their practice field, where Coach Gamble and Coach Benning were already huddled at home plate over their clipboards. "Hot sauce. Oh well. Hey, your home run against that pitcher should make them think twice about keeping you on the bench."

"I wish!"

The two friends entered the dugout, which was busy with boys unloading their equipment bags. At the far end of the dugout Chris sat, sulking. Dirk removed a bat from his bag, noticed Jalen and Daniel, and nudged Chris before pointing their way. Chris slowly turned his head and directed a hateful glare at Jalen.

"Yeah, you did this." Chris used his left hand to raise his right arm so they could clearly see his elbow packed in ice beneath a thick and tightly wrapped Ace bandage.

It was Daniel who answered Chris. "Stop making excuses. Your arm—or your nerve—fizzed out. That Bronxville pitcher's didn't, and we lost. Stuff happens."

Chris glanced at Daniel but directed his angry scowl at Jalen, as if he'd been the one who'd popped off about the Bronxville pitcher.

"My arm doesn't give out," Chris snarled, "unless some jerk smacks it when I'm in the middle of throwing something."

"Serves you right," Daniel snapped, "for tossing his dad's sandwiches in the garbage."

"I've had about enough of you." Dirk pointed his bat at Daniel.

Daniel snorted with contempt to show he was unafraid before marching out of the dugout.

Dirk then directed his bat at Jalen. "And we've got a surprise for you."

"What surprise?" Daniel asked.

"Oh, you'll see." Chris's voice was laced with pure evil, and the light in his eyes held Jalen's attention the way they say a cobra can hypnotize its prey.

24

THE HARSH BLAST OF COACH GAMBLE'S WHISTLE broke the trance.

Jalen dumped his gear bag behind the bench, whipped out his glove, and headed toward home plate at a jog.

"Okay, take a knee," said Coach Gamble in his gruff voice. "First of all, that was absolute crap yesterday. The Rockton Rockets aren't about second place. Right, Coach?"

Coach Benning's mouth was full of sunflower seeds, but he nodded vigorously in agreement.

"That's right." Coach Gamble answered his own question. "And I'm sure most of you—if not all of you—saw that Chris is hurt. The doctor said it looks like he sprained his elbow and we have no idea how long it will take to heal, so we are going to have to work ten times as hard this week if we are going to be ready for the Boston tournament next weekend."

Jalen expected Coach Gamble to give him a dirty look, but it was just the opposite. Coach Gamble looked around at his team, not making eye contact with Jalen at all. This seemed worse than a dirty look.

No one said a word, and finally Coach Gamble glanced down at his clipboard before announcing that they would have practices on Tuesday and Thursday evenings.

"And we'll be leaving for Boston at seven a.m. on Friday morning. Now let's not have a good practice, let's have a great practice!" The coach blew his whistle and the team began its warm-up by running bases.

During long throw, Jalen saw Chris staring at him from the dugout like an angry troll. After a while, he forgot about Chris. He'd shifted his entire focus to baseball and worked up a sweat shagging balls, scrambling for pop flies, and swinging his bat relentlessly in the tee and soft-toss drills. It did seem to him, as practice progressed, that no one was speaking to him but Daniel. Coach Gamble and Coach Benning had no comments on his efforts, good or bad, and his teammates stared dead-faced at him, if they looked his way at all.

Jalen worked so hard and with such intensity that he

had no idea how big a problem he really had until their water break before live batting practice, when Caleb Paquet brushed up against him.

"Hey." Caleb spoke in a whisper.

When Jalen looked at him, Caleb was very busy with a knot in his glove lace.

"Me?" Jalen asked, also quietly.

"Yup," Caleb said without looking up. "I just want to say sorry."

"For what?" The water in Jalen's stomach seemed to go sour.

"It's nothing personal," Caleb said. "This whole thing is not my idea."

Caleb began to walk away, but Jalen caught his arm and asked, "Are you saying sorry because no one is talking to me?"

"No." Caleb shook free and spoke through his teeth. He gave Jalen an angry look that didn't match his words of apology. "I'm sorry for what I'm *about* to do."

25

JALEN BEGAN THE LIVE HITTING PERIOD IN THE outfield.

His eyes got lost in the tattered clouds above, like he was searching for something to appear, some shape or sign, as he thought about Caleb's warning. It seemed like some sort of practical joke to make him uneasy. Maybe that was all it was.

Daniel was pitching when Caleb smacked a ball Jalen's way. Because he hadn't been focused on the action, Jalen missed the pop fly. He threw the ball in to Daniel, wondering if a fly ball was the thing Caleb had been talking about. It didn't make sense, though. How could Caleb have known Jalen would miss the ball? Also, was that really something to apologize for?

Jalen spent the rest of the session wondering, until it was his turn to bat. He realized Caleb was now on the mound. No one spoke as Jalen stepped up to the plate. Birds chattered in the trees above. New leaves whispered what might have been a warning. Jalen took a practice swing and set his feet.

Caleb flexed his arm and went into his windup.

The pitch came in, fast and wild. Dirk Benning had to leap up and away to snag it. The cloud of dust from Dirk's efforts settled around the plate. Each batter got ten pitches to hit, and Jalen frowned, thinking that Caleb might have been instructed not to give him a pitch he could hit.

"Looking a little out of control, Caleb!" Coach Gamble shouted from where he stood leaning up against the dugout. "Let's see some control!"

Jalen was briefly confused, because maybe he was wrong.

He tightened his grip on the bat and set his feet again. Out on the mound Caleb had his lower lip between his teeth. He took a deep breath and went into his windup.

This time the ball came directly at Jalen. He dropped to the dirt just in time.

"Caleb!" Coach Gamble shouted. "I told you to get control!"

While Jalen heard what Coach Gamble said, what he saw was Chris grinning from the shadows of the dugout. Then he heard Dirk snickering from behind his catcher's mask and he knew what Caleb had apologized for—a beanball.

Jalen kept his chin up. He dusted himself off and took his place in the batter's box once again. His own face was deadpan. He wasn't going to give anyone the satisfaction of knowing he was upset.

The next pitch was wide and high again, and Coach Gamble chewed on Caleb's ear. Jalen was determined to make contact with the ball just to show them that he wasn't afraid.

The next pitch was high and very tight, but Jalen kept his hands inside the ball and pulled a liner right over the bag at third.

"That's it, Jalen!" Daniel shouted from his spot at second base, confirming for Jalen that at least one person was still on his side.

Coach Gamble yelled, "Paquet, tighten up. You've got to get a lot better for Boston."

In response, Caleb sent two throws right down the middle. The first surprised Jalen so much that he swung and missed, but the second he got hold of and sent over the fence. Daniel crowed from second base, but other than that, the only encouragement Jalen got was from the birds. He settled in for the next pitch, determined to send another one over.

When the pitch came, it was fast and straight at his head.

The helmet's faceguard took the hit. However, Jalen still saw stars and staggered to keep his feet.

26

COACH GAMBLE WAS THE FIRST TO REACH HIM,
upset and concerned. Jalen thought whatever had been
planned must have been the work of Chris and Dirk
alone. Coach Gamble helped him to the dugout and got
a bag of ice.

"Let's see if we can keep your jaw from swelling too
much," the coach said anxiously.

Coach Benning hustled over and started asking Jalen
questions. "Where are we? What day is it?" Jalen's face
hurt, but his mind was clear. He answered easily.

When Coach Gamble saw his son grinning, he snapped,
"You think that's funny? I ought to throw a baseball at
your mouth and see if you're still smiling."

The light went out of Chris's face and he stared straight ahead, muttering to himself.

Jalen was still answering questions when Coach Gamble yelled at the pitcher. "Caleb, come here! Daniel, take the mound!"

Caleb moved reluctantly toward the dugout. He exchanged the quickest of looks with Chris before asking, "What, Coach?"

"That's what I'm asking you: What?" the coach said. "What's going on?"

Caleb shrugged and rubbed his elbow. "Not sure, Coach. Too many pitches yesterday? All of a sudden my fastball's getting away from me."

"What do you think you should say to Jalen?" the coach asked.

Caleb looked at the ground. "Sorry, Jalen."

"It's okay," Jalen said. "I wasn't expecting it, that's all."

After Jalen counted backward from thirty and showed no trouble with his balance, Coach Benning said, "At least he doesn't have a concussion, but we better get his dad here to take him home."

"I'll be okay, really," Jalen said, not wanting them to call the Silver Liner and upset his father. "Mr. Bellone is taking me home."

The coaches hovered with concern, changing the ice

pack and watching Jalen until practice ended.

Jalen's teammates, spooked by the turn of events, continued to avoid him. Coach Gamble dismissed them all with his typical gruff comments and a warning about being on time Tuesday.

Giving Jalen instructions to ice his cheek when he got home and to call immediately if he got a headache or double vision, the coaches let him go.

Jalen and Daniel were halfway across the parking lot before either of them spoke.

"I'm glad that's over with," said Jalen.

"Practice?" Daniel asked.

"No, Chris's revenge."

"Revenge? Chris?" Daniel looked confused. "You mean Caleb wasn't the one who thought up the beanball?"

Jalen nodded.

Daniel stopped and his mouth fell open. "That came from Chris? How do you know?"

"Caleb actually told me," Jalen said. "He apologized before he even did it, and before that Chris and Dirk said they had a surprise for me."

Daniel looked back at the dugout, narrowed his eyes, and balled his hands into fists. "I got something for those fatheads. I can't believe it. That is such hot sauce."

Jalen grabbed him by the arm. "Just leave it, Daniel."

"Leave it?" Daniel's eyes widened. "You can't just let them do that to you."

"Sometimes the best thing to do is let things go. I've learned that."

"Well, I haven't."

Daniel's father gave his truck horn a beep.

"Come on, your dad's waiting." Jalen headed for the truck. Its bed was loaded up with fresh green hay. The back of the extended cab smelled like manure and sun-baked grass.

Daniel's father wore a sweat-stained cowboy hat tilted back on his head. His hands were calloused and cracked, with dirt under his fingernails. He looked at Jalen in sur-prise. "What happened to him?" he asked.

Daniel told the story about the beanballs.

"They did that to you?" Daniel's father looked at Jalen in the rearview mirror, studying his face.

Jalen held up his hand to hide his cheek and said, "It was an accident."

"No," said Daniel. "It was on purpose."

Jalen angled away and kept quiet, even when Daniel's father stopped the truck so that he could turn around in his seat to see Jalen directly. His dark brown eyes burned with fury. His face hardened, stonelike. It was as if the older man was suddenly possessed by a demon, and Jalen knew where Daniel got his temper from.

If Daniel was ready to fight, Jalen didn't even want to think about what his father was going to do.

27

"DID THEY?" MR. BELLONE DEMANDED. "DID THEY
do what Daniel said?"

Jalen stopped trying to hide the swollen side of his face
and said, "It happened, but I can't prove anything. He said
he was sorry."

Jalen locked eyes with Daniel's father until the fire suddenly went out.

"Yeah, that's how they do it." Daniel's father sniffed,
turned around, and put the truck back into gear. He spoke
as he drove, without looking back. "You got the right idea
just letting it go. There's us and there's them, and it's
always good to know the difference."

"But we're all on the same *team*, Dad," said Daniel.

"Maybe the same *baseball* team," his dad said, "but that's not what I'm talking about. Jalen knows, don't you, Jalen?"

Jalen nodded to Daniel's dad in the mirror that he did, and it seemed to cast a gloom on the three of them, so that they rode to the stables where Daniel's family lived in silence.

They pulled through the towering gates of Mount Tipton, the enormous estate owned by Cat's stepfather. Daniel's father drove up the long, winding drive through the tall trees and past the stables so he could back his truck up to one of the barns.

"Daniel, I could use your help unloading this hay," Daniel's father said.

"Aw, Dad, we're going up to the big house to watch the game with Cat. She's waiting for us and it already started."

"We'll help you first, Mr. Bellone," Jalen said.

Daniel gave Jalen a dirty look, but he left his gear bag in the truck and fell in alongside him. They began to lift the big, scratchy bales off the truck bed and heave them into the barn, where Daniel's father stacked them, using a baling hook. It took them no more than fifteen minutes. Mr. Bellone thanked them, and Jalen thanked him for the ride.

As they trudged up toward the mansion, Daniel complained, "Now I'm all sweaty."

"You were sweaty anyway," said Jalen.

"Goody Two-shoes."

"Which means what, exactly?" Jalen asked.

"It's a nice name for a brownnoser, which means—"

"I know what 'brownnoser' means!" Jalen said. "I was talking about Goody Two-shoes. It's one of those things people say, like 'hot sauce.'"

"Hot sauce can be really good, or really bad, depending on the situation." Daniel loved to talk about his favorite expression. "Bad is if you get it up your nose or in your eyes somehow. Good is when it's on a taco with lots of sour cream. Then nothing is better."

"I don't mind helping your dad," Jalen said, changing the subject. "I appreciate all the rides he and your mom give me."

"It's nothing." Daniel dismissed their rides with a wave of his hand. "They gotta take me anyway."

They circled the mansion and knocked at the door to the kitchen. A maid let them in and told them Cat was waiting in the TV room.

"Shh," Cat said, waving for them to sit down without looking up. "JY is up."

They sat down on either side of her. Daniel settled into the deep cushions of the long, low couch, but Jalen sat on the edge of his seat with his knees pressing into the coffee table. The sixty-inch screen on the wall in front of them was filled with the image of James Yager at the plate, taking a practice swing. The volume was low, but Jalen could hear the excitement in the voices of the announcers as they discussed Yager's incredible hitting streak and how it had revived his career.

On the mound was Josh Tomlin. They sat frozen while Tomlin threw three cutters for a 1–2 count.

"I told you he needed you," Cat said without taking her eyes from the screen. She clenched her hands so hard they shook.

Jalen bit his lip and forgot about his swollen jaw.

Tomlin wound up and threw his next pitch, a sinker.

JY hit a three-hopper deep to short and just beat the throw to take first base.

The announcers went wild.

The camera cut to a pair of fans in Yankee gear going crazy amid a sea of Cleveland supporters.

Jalen felt sick.

28

YAGER ENDED THE NIGHT WITH TWO SINGLES AND
two strikeouts.

The Yankees won 3–2.

Cat shut down the TV and let the remote clatter onto the coffee table. "Well, he sure didn't bat a thousand."

"Yeah, who needs a .500 hitter?" Daniel's voice was full of sarcasm.

Cat turned to see Jalen's reaction.

"Tell me you don't feel as bad as you look." Cat put a hand on his shoulder. "You gonna tell me what happened to your jaw now?"

Jalen told her how Chris had somehow convinced Caleb to throw beanballs at him.

"That stinks," she said.

"Now this." Jalen pointed at the TV.

"Don't look so down," Cat said, jumping up and popping the top of a pizza box. "Have another piece of pizza. Want another soda?"

Her false cheer made Jalen feel worse. "I've had enough. I better get home." He stood up to go.

"Here, can I see that?" Cat reached for Jalen's iPhone. "Let's get your Twitter going. How about something like . . . 'JY has another super night! Looks like it's still #LUCKYCALAMARI.' Look, you've already got fifty-two followers. This is gonna take off!"

Cat had set up a Twitter account on Jalen's phone during the commercial breaks under the name CalamariKid1. She had given him some basic instructions, but he was confused by it all, and not up for even thinking about it now.

"Hey, it's one game," Cat said. "Wait until he goes O-fer against the Klubot."

Jalen had to admit that the thought of JY being shut down by Corey Kluber the next night let a small ray of hope into his gloomy mood. The light quickly faded, though. He thanked Cat and dropped Daniel off at his place before continuing down the driveway and on down Old Post Road by himself. It was dark, and the idea of rooting against JY seemed so wrong, he decided against it.

He took the iPhone out of his pocket and dialed Cat.

"You okay?" was how she answered.

"Not really," he said. "I'm not rooting against JY anymore. I'm wishing him to strike out, then I tweet about how great his night was? It just feels wrong."

"It's business, Jalen."

"It is and it isn't." Jalen saw a car coming, and he stepped off the road to let it pass. "This whole thing happened because I love baseball. I love the Yankees. I love JY, and I love to play the game. I've got to focus on that, my own game. My dad's restaurant is taking off already, so he doesn't need all this JY tweeting stuff anymore. This whole baseball genius thing is over, and I've just got to face it and move on."

He decided to tell her about his mom, how he wanted to find her, and how the money could help.

"Wow," she said.

Another car zipped past and Jalen continued his trek toward town. He could see the lights now flickering below him through the trees. "I guess that's over now."

"But I don't think it *is* over." Cat was pleading with him. "One good night is not going to fix things for JY, not with Jeffrey Foxx it's not."

"See? Now we're on *that* guy's side?" Jalen said. "No thanks, Cat. That's not even like you."

"We're on our own side, Jalen. You've got a gift. You should use it. You should get paid for it. People should know about it. . . . Your mother should know."

Jalen trudged around a bend without speaking.

"Jalen? You there?"

"Yeah," he said.

"I'm sorry if I said something wrong."

"It's okay," he said. "My life is a mess, Cat, but at least my dad's happy."

"You're going to be happy too, Jalen. I know it."

"Just like you knew JY would blow it tonight against Cleveland?"

It was Cat's turn to be quiet. Jalen began to pass some houses, and he stepped onto the sidewalk.

"I could have worked for five hundred dollars a game," Jalen finally said. "But now I don't think even that's on the table."

"You're worth twenty times that." Cat's voice was flat and without apology. "If you want to make it big, you gotta think big, Jalen. That much I do know."

Jalen hit the center of town. He crossed the street and rounded the corner at the train station. "Well, I'm back at the Silver Liner. I'm gonna go in and talk to my dad. Thanks again for the pizza."

"Anytime. See you tomorrow, Jalen."

"See you."

He crossed the parking lot and paused to hold the door for two couples coming out. They wore smiles and chatted about how good their meal had been. Inside, the restaurant was bustling. Greta had on the same dress she'd worn the night before. Her hair was frazzled, but she smiled at Jalen as she led two customers toward a table in the back.

He found his father in the kitchen amid the clatter of plates and the clash of pans. Food sizzled on the stove, and the rich smells of red sauce, onions, fish, and sausages filled the air. The kitchen was busy with assistants dressed in aprons, hairnets, and paper hats.

"Jalen!" His father slipped a golden fish filet out of a crackling pan and onto a plate before setting it down and hugging his son. "What a night! How was you practice? Did the Yankees win?"

"Okay, yeah, they won."

"Jalen, what happen to your face?" His father scowled as he placed two fingers on Jalen's chin, turning his face toward the light.

"Nothing, Dad." Jalen shrugged free. "Just a wild pitch. It happens. I'm fine."

"I thought baseball, she's safe." Jalen's dad clucked his tongue, still troubled.

Jalen talked his father out of his worry. He was relieved

when his dad brightened, wagged his head toward the office, and said, "Come here. I gotta tell you something in private."

"Private?"

"Yeah. It's a good thing." His father led him into the tiny office and closed the door on his noisy kitchen.

"A good thing?" Jalen sat down in the rickety chair beside his father's desk.

His father sat down too. He massaged his bald head before placing his elbows on his knees and leaning toward Jalen. "No, actually, is a *great* thing."

29

JALEN'S DAD POINTED IN THE DIRECTION OF THE
dining room. "You see two men wearing the suits at table
seven when you come in?"

"There were a lot of people."

"Don't worry. Maybe they gone now, but they are from
Goldman Sachs, and they say to me, they say, 'Fabio, the
Silver Liner, she's a brilliant idea and everybody is talking
about her.' They say I should franchise."

"Franchise?" Jalen remembered Cat talking about a
franchise.

"You know, restaurants everywhere, like Burger
King, like Applebee's, only nice like the Capital Grille."
His father's blue eyes sparkled with delight. "They said

they got people who do this all the time, and they got the money. Jalen, we gonna be so rich, maybe famous, too. Like Wolfgang Puck."

Jalen now felt like a yo-yo, up and down, up and down.

"Jalen, you look tired." His father patted his hand. "You go home and get to sleep. I'm gonna be late again tonight. Let me get you some ice."

"You sure you don't need me to help?" Jalen followed his dad out into the kitchen.

"No, I got plenty of people." His father dumped a scoopful of ice from the cooler into a plastic bag, tied it, and handed it to his son.

Then Greta burst through the swinging door and threw her hands into the air. "They just keep coming."

Jalen's dad only laughed and yanked the next order off its clip before turning toward his stoves.

Jalen let himself out the back and went straight home. He got ready for bed and hopped in without bothering to even look at his mother's picture. He had enough discomfort with the swelling on his jaw. He didn't need a heartache on top of it all.

In the morning his father's eyes were red from lack of sleep, but he wore a smile that brightened even Jalen's day. His dad made them breakfast, then headed off to the market. Daniel was waiting for Jalen in the back of the bus.

"How was the restaurant last night?" Daniel asked.

"Great." Jalen bumped fists with his friend and sat down beside him. "I guess some Goldman guys want to turn it into a franchise, like McDonald's, only nicer."

"Sweet," Daniel said. "How's the face? It looks a little swollen."

"It's fine."

"So, I got something I want to show you." Daniel held up a finger, then dug into his backpack. He came up with a Ziploc bag that contained what looked like about a dozen Cocoa Puffs cereal balls.

"Cereal?" Jalen said.

Daniel studied the contents of the Ziploc. "Kinda looks like that, doesn't it? I'll save that for another day, but for today I thought I'd sprinkle these bad boys inside Chris's backpack. See, they're not cereal. They're rabbit turds."

"Whaaat?"

Daniel chuckled. "Yeah, they look kind of harmless, but man do they stink when you flatten them. So, when his books shift around a bit, squish, squish, bang. El stinko. Then he fishes around in there and there's rabbit poop all over his fingers. He might even puke."

"What brought this on?"

"You serious?" Daniel scrunched up his face. "No way are we letting him get away with those beanballs yesterday."

"He didn't throw them," Jalen said.

"No, he only got Caleb to do it. That's just as bad, maybe worse." Daniel tucked the Ziploc carefully back inside his own backpack. "It stinks is all I know, so I got some stink for him to enjoy."

"I don't know," Jalen said.

"You don't have to know. You just have to be the lookout for me."

"Now I'm a part of it?" Jalen asked.

"That's what makes it a valid payback." Daniel gave him a short nod.

"He'll know."

"He'll *suspect*, but he won't know." Daniel frowned. "Look, I'm doing it with or without you. I can't look at your face and just sit on my hands."

Jalen stayed quiet for the rest of the ride.

As they left the bus, he asked, "How are you gonna do it?"

"That's my boy. I knew you weren't gonna let your BFF go it alone." The two of them fell into the crowd, kids swarming up the steps and into the school like salmon swimming up a river.

"I didn't say . . ." Just then Jalen saw Chris up ahead of them, shoving a scrawny kid who played clarinet in the school band face-first into the brick wall outside the entrance.

"Okay," Jalen said, "tell me what I have to do."

30

THE PLAN WAS FOR EACH OF THEM TO GET A BATH-
room pass at nine thirty, right in the middle of second
period. They weren't in the same class, so it wouldn't be
obvious. When the clock's big hand hit the six, Jalen asked
for the bathroom pass. His history teacher, Mr. Ingles,
gave him a sour look, but nodded toward the wooden pass
hanging from a key chain on a hook just inside the door.

Jalen took it and hurried through the empty hallways to
the bathroom closest to Chris's locker. Daniel was already
there.

"Where you been?" Daniel asked in an intense whisper.

"It's nine thirty."

"It was nine thirty three minutes ago." Daniel marched

past Jalen. He poked his head out into the hall and looked both ways. "Okay. Come on, let's go."

Jalen followed.

"You stay here and watch both ways." Daniel pointed to a spot where one hallway T-boned another.

"What should I do?" Jalen said. "I can't just stand here."

"Pretend you're tying your shoe. Bang a locker if you see someone."

Jalen bent down and untied his shoe, thinking of an excuse for being someplace that was clearly not on the path from his class to the bathroom.

Daniel got to Chris's locker and looked back. Jalen gave him a thumbs-up, then watched as Daniel slipped a small screwdriver from his pocket and jammed it into the edge of the locker. Daniel had discovered the way to open the lockers early in the year, when his own locker had given him trouble with the combination. Daniel fussed with the screwdriver for a few seconds, then looked up again, making an *okay* sign. Jalen looked around again and signaled *okay*.

Daniel popped the locker with his elbow and the door crashed open.

Jalen's heart thumped against his ribs as Daniel fumbled with Chris's backpack. He yanked it out of the locker, zipped it open, fiddled with something inside that Jalen couldn't see, then removed the Ziploc of rabbit turds from his front pants pocket and dumped the contents into the backpack. A cackle of laughter escaped Daniel as he jiggled the back-pack to settle the turds into its depths. Jalen felt giddy, and he giggled to himself until he looked down the hallway he was supposed to be watching and saw Dr. Menkin, the prin-cipal, marching toward him with a disapproving scowl.

Jalen panicked and banged his fist against a locker sev-eral times.

Daniel turned with a look of disbelief—as if he expected Jalen was trying to scare him as a joke—that quickly turned to horror when he realized that Jalen's warning was for real. Daniel began stuffing the backpack into the locker.

Jalen looked back at Dr. Menkin, who was now approach-ing on a double-time march.

Unless Jalen outright tackled the principal, Daniel would never make it.

31

JALEN THREW HIS SHOULDERS BACK AND HEADED
for the principal.

Dr. Menkin was looking beyond Jalen, sensing the situation with the intuition of a twenty-year educator with a PhD. Jalen stepped right, then left, directly in the principal's path. Dr. Menkin bounced off Jalen but kept his feet, slipped past, and stood staring down the hallway Jalen had been guarding.

"Are you going to tell me what's going on here, Mr. DeLuca?" Dr. Menkin gave Jalen an angry look.

The principal caught Jalen by the arm and marched him around the corner. Daniel was nowhere to be seen.

"Someone has been stealing money from the lockers all year. Never in my life did I think it was you."

"I didn't take anything, Dr. Menkin," Jalen pleaded.

"Why were you blocking me?"

"I—I tried to get out of the way," Jalen said. "I got nervous because I was supposed to be using the bathroom, but I stepped outside for some air and I was on my way back to class."

Jalen still held the wooden bathroom pass in one hand, but he turned his pockets inside out, producing nothing except a worn-down pencil. "I didn't take anything. See?"

The principal studied his empty pockets, and his expression seemed to soften. "I saw all that stuff about you and James Yager over the weekend."

"Yeah," Jalen said, "it's been great for my dad's business."

"Well, you're lucky I'm a big Yankees fan." The principal tilted his head. "Lucky calamari, huh?"

"Kind of." Jalen didn't know what else to say.

"Okay, I'll have to get some." The principal motioned with his head. "Get back to class."

Jalen practically skipped down the hallways, he was so giddy over having escaped a close call. Daniel was giddy too when they met in science class the very next period.

"Good job, amigo!" Daniel slapped him a high five.

"What are you two up to?" asked Cat, setting her books down on the lab table in front of them.

"Just delivering presents from the Easter bunny," said Daniel.

"Easter bunny? What, like chocolate eggs?" asked Cat.

"Something like that." Daniel began to giggle. "Anyway, I don't want to tell you too much because I don't want to ruin the surprise you're going to get at lunch."

Cat looked at Jalen. "What's wrong with him?"

"A lot," Jalen said.

Science class was a yawn because they spent most of it helping their teacher catalog his equipment for next year's sixth-grade class. But lunch came after that, and Jalen had to admit he was excited to see the result of Daniel's devious deed.

32

CHRIS HAD HIS ARM IN A SLING.

Jalen wondered how necessary it was, or, as Daniel insisted was the case, if he was simply continuing to support his excuse for flopping in the championship game against Bronxville. Jalen, Cat, and Daniel all sat down on the end of a table just across the main aisle from Chris and his bunch.

"Watch this," Daniel said, angling his head toward Chris.

Chris used his left hand to open his lunch bag and dig down into it for a sandwich. He stopped talking and his face got a funny look. When he pulled his hand out of the bag several little brown rabbit turds popped out and rolled across the table. Several others were smeared onto his fingers in a brown and putrid yellow mess.

Chris's face went from confusion to horror. Instinctively, he sniffed his soiled hand. With a bark, he exploded up out of his seat. His chair screeched across the floor, but before he could take a step, he gagged and vomited on the lunch table. The wet slick spatter flowed like a tide, spilling from the table's edge in brown sheets to the floor.

Everyone within thirty feet issued a collective groan. "Ewww!"

Daniel craned his neck and casually observed, "Looks like he had bacon for breakfast."

Dirk, who'd been sprayed by the blast, staggered to his feet, slipped in the puke puddle, went down like a dynamited building, and was barely able to get to his knees before a gusher of barf spewed from his own mouth. Another universal groan filled the air, this time punctuated with little horrified yelps from various girls who weren't used to such spectacles.

There was some nervous laughter, but most kids reacted with a mixture of horror and disgust. Daniel bit back a grin and trembled with the effort it took not to burst into celebration. He snickered to himself and looked down. "Oh, that's too much. That's just too perfect."

Jalen wiped the smile off his own face several times

and disguised his glee with several fake coughs. Cat wore a look of genuine sympathy, but that was just Cat. Even though she knew Chris was a big jerk, she'd still feel bad about him being sick and embarrassed.

"You did that?" she said in a hushed voice, leaning toward Daniel across the table.

"*We* did that." Daniel gave Jalen a satisfied look. "You know those bunnies you see all over the lawns in Mount Tipton? Well, their poop has to go somewhere."

"You dumped them in his lunch bag. Wow," said Jalen, impressed.

A custodian showed up with a mop and a bucket and began to clean up the mess as Dirk and Chris stumbled off toward the bathroom. The sharp smell of disinfectant cleaner cut into the sour scent of vomit.

"That's really disgusting," Cat said.

"So is that." Daniel pointed to Jalen's swollen jaw.

Cat frowned and looked at Jalen. "True."

"I look that bad?" Jalen's heart sank.

"No." Cat giggled. "That they did it is disgusting. It'd be hard for *you* to look bad, Jalen."

"Aw, man." Daniel paused as he removed a sandwich from his own lunch bag. "Who needs rabbit poop? 'Oh, Jalen, you're so cute.' You're making *me* barf."

"I didn't say 'cute.'" Cat turned to Jalen.

Jalen felt his face heat up, and he changed the subject, even though he was delighted by Cat's attention. "So, we gonna watch the game together again tonight?"

"You guys are welcome," Cat said, taking out a small tub of yogurt and digging in. "I'll have my mom order some more pizza, and we can celebrate."

"Celebrate?" Jalen asked.

Cat's eyes were aglow. "Tonight it's going to happen. I was checking out Kluber's stats at breakfast this morning. I'm telling you, JY is going to be texting me before he leaves the locker room tonight. He's gonna be begging to get you back."

33

JALEN HELPED HIS DAD AFTER SCHOOL.

There were a lot of new faces at the Silver Liner, and the ones who'd been around carried themselves more upright and their faces seemed to glow with pride. The Silver Liner had gone from a dumpy diner-restaurant struggling for survival to a superstar restaurant with talk of its special stuffed calamari on everyone's lips because it was a big part of a sports miracle. Jalen wondered how people would react if they thought the miracle was fading.

As he shelled shrimp, folded napkins, and set out knives and forks on the tables, Jalen checked his phone from time to time, following the tweets about JY's performance the night before. People were definitely talking about the Silver Liner, urging JY to get back there ASAP and to consider taking some stuffed calamari on the road next time. Jalen smiled to himself, knowing that the real secret would be for JY to take *him* on the road.

When he took some garbage out and opened the Dumpster, the smell reminded him about the circus with Chris in the lunchroom. Jalen wondered if it would make things worse or better at tomorrow night's practice. He'd get a hint in school. If Chris gave him dirty looks, he could probably plan on more beanballs. He wondered how long he could endure it, and that started him thinking for the hundredth time about escaping to Bronxville. There had to be a way to convince the coach to take Daniel, so they could both go. What would happen if Coach Allen knew Jalen was a baseball genius and could use his skills to help the Bandits win?

With all the preparation for the evening complete, Jalen's dad insisted that the two of them share an early meal before Jalen went to Cat's house. They sat on stools at the countertop where his father did most of his work. There was still hustle and bustle all around them, but the steaming plates of linguine and clams set out on two sides of the corner made it somehow seem like a private meal. His father looked weary, but he still had the twinkle in his eyes that told Jalen he was overjoyed.

"You're not tired, Dad?"

"Maybe a little." His dad sighed deeply but looked around and grinned. "But this is what I love. A busy restaurant, and the people complaining they can't get a table until next month. I take the walk-ins at the end of the night, and they keep coming later and later."

"How are you going to franchise? You can't be at every restaurant at once." Jalen shoveled in a mouthful of food.

"Once I get everybody doing what I need them to do, I can teach more people to do it again. Then the people I train, they train more people. You do it like this for a while and soon fifty Silver Liners!"

"But isn't it your cooking that everyone wants?" Jalen asked.

His father shrugged. "Is my cooking, yes, but a lot of the people can cook like me. The secret is *nonna*'s recipes and making the sauce just like she make it. And also, the seafood's gotta be fresh. Most people, they don't want to take the time anymore. They hurry the sauce. They take the seafood even when it's not perfect."

"I like seeing you smile, Dad."

"You're happy too, right?" his dad asked.

"If you get rich and famous, can we find my mom?" Jalen felt uncomfortable asking, but it was too late to take it back. His father's face went from shock to embarrassment, and Jalen couldn't remember seeing his dad embarrassed before.

"Your mom?" His father's embarrassment turned to pain.

34

JALEN'S DAD SLID OFF HIS STOOL AND BACKED
away. "I don't know, Jalen. I don't know. I . . . I gotta check
the marinara sauce."

Jalen set down his fork and watched his father work
over the stove. He regretted bringing up the subject of
his mom. He knew better. It had become an unwritten
rule between them. She was there in her picture on his
dresser, but talking about her always upset his dad, and
Jalen never wanted to do that.

"Dad," he called through the noisy kitchen. "I'm sorry."

His father dusted his hands and wiped them on his
apron as he turned around, smiling again. "How you lik-
ing the phone? Good, no?"

"I like it." Jalen nodded, eager to put distance between them and the subject of his mom. "I like Twitter and knowing what's going on. People are telling JY he needs to get back and get some lucky calamari."

"I got it for him when he is ready." Jalen's dad puffed up his chest and patted it.

His dad sat back down. They ate without talking before picking up their plates and rinsing them in the giant sink. Jalen's dad gave him a hug and a kiss. It was as if the subject of Jalen's mother had never been raised. "You have fun with your friends!"

"Thanks, Dad." Jalen left through the front, glad he and his dad could just put uncomfortable things behind them. It would have been nice if his father had responded in a more positive way, eager to help, maybe even excited by the prospect. But Jalen should have known better. Besides the silent photograph in his room, and a rare uncomfortable mention, it was as if he had no mother.

As he walked out, he was aware of how different the restaurant looked with its crisp white tablecloths and napkins and the handful of waiters and waitresses ready to go. It raised Jalen's spirits to think that things could be so quickly transformed. As he slogged along uphill toward Cat's house, he thought about the things in his life that weren't right and how they could be fixed. JY needing him again could change a lot. He could have money to hire a detective. His dad would never have to know. If he could get JY to tell people about his genius, he could use that to get Daniel a spot on the Bronxville team. It could all happen.

He just needed Kluber to 0-fer JY.

Cat and Daniel were waiting for him in the TV room at the back of the mansion. Jalen could smell the warm pizza resting in its box on the coffee table. The game was about to begin.

"You ready?" Cat asked. "Pizza?"

"You know my dad. I just ate." He sat next to Cat and reached across her to bump fists with Daniel.

"Kluber is a killer," Daniel said.

"We'll see." Jalen's mouth felt dry, but his clenched hands were wet.

The first two Yankees batters struck out before Sánchez hit an easy pop fly into left field, ending the top of the inning. Watching the Yankees on defense was painfully slow for Jalen. All he cared about was the next at bat for his team. JY was set to bat sixth, so they'd get an idea where he was in the second inning for sure. Finally, the inning ended with Cleveland taking a 1–0 lead.

Jalen stood up and paced the room during the commercials. Daniel glanced at him nervously, but Cat sat ramrod straight with her arms folded across her chest, wearing a confident smile.

Tollerson stepped up to the plate for the Yankees and drilled a line drive through the 5–6 hole for a double. Tyler Hutt hit a single, putting runners on first and third and affording JY a nice opportunity. Kluber looked calm and cool, but suddenly not so dominant as Yager boldly took the plate.

"Just my luck," Jalen muttered.

"We'll see." Cat's eyes hadn't lost their sparkle.

JY took a few practice swings and set his feet. Kluber wound up and threw a fastball high and outside. JY tagged it. The ball took off for the fences.

Jalen felt his stomach drop, but the ball tailed off and went outside the right foul pole.

"Wow," Daniel said. "Close."

Kluber wound up again, this time throwing his curveball. JY swung and missed.

Jalen pumped his fist, feeling guilty but unable to keep from smiling.

"0–2," said Cat.

"He's got to throw another curve." Jalen spoke without thinking.

Kluber did throw a curve and JY whiffed.

"Yes!" Cat and Jalen slapped high fives.

Daniel frowned.

"Hey, this is what we want," Cat told him.

"I know. It just feels weird to be so excited."

Weird or not, that was how things went for JY and the Yankees, who lost 5–2 with JY batting 0-fer on the night. At the end of the game, the announcers jokingly discussed how James Yager definitely needed to get back to New York for some lucky calamari.

The three friends stood when it was over. The pizza box sat open and empty, except for several crusts that Cat didn't want.

"Now what?" Daniel asked.

"We wait," Cat said.

"Tomorrow's the last day of school." Jalen wanted to change the subject. Waiting would be agony. He hated even to think about it.

"Hard to believe, right?" Cat said. "Next year, seventh grade."

"Talk about old," Daniel said.

"You gonna walk out with me?" Jalen asked him.

"Sure."

Cat saw them to the kitchen door, and they stepped outside. The air had a slight chill to it, but Jalen felt like the shiver in his spine had more to do with his excitement over JY's flop than the cold. The three of them bumped fists, but as Jalen and Daniel turned to go, Cat's phone chimed. Jalen didn't want to give it a jinx, but he couldn't help the hope that flooded him as Cat checked her phone for the text.

"That's not JY, is it?" Daniel said.

"Yes," Cat said, "it is."

Cat's face glowed in the light of her phone, but Jalen couldn't read her expression as she thrust the phone at him.

"Take a look at this."

35

"WHAT'S IT MEAN?" JALEN HELD ON TO THE phone, reading the words again.

"Just what it says," Cat replied. "He wants to talk when he gets back. He means talk about the terms of your deal."

"He didn't say that, though."

Cat took her phone back from him and glanced at it before stuffing it into her jeans pocket. "He doesn't have to. It's self-explanatory. He realizes he's not going to get that new contract extension the way he's going."

Jalen's heart thumped inside his chest. "But maybe not. Maybe it's something else."

"Don't be afraid of success." Cat waved her hand to dismiss his doubts. "Or of me being right all the time."

She huffed on her nails and polished them on her sweatshirt.

"Oh, brother," Daniel said. "What a load of hot sauce."

"Does the truth hurt so much?" she asked.

"If your head swells any more," Daniel said, "you'll turn into a hot-air balloon and float away."

"When a guy's right all the time," Cat said, "he's a genius, but when a girl's right, she's got a swollen head? Talk about hot sauce. . . ."

"I gotta go, guys." Jalen turned and left them to their bickering. He marched downhill, feeling light on his feet. The game couldn't have gone better for him, which meant worse for JY. He passed the Silver Liner parking lot, bursting with cars, and crunched down the gravel drive to his house.

The last day of school always had a partylike atmosphere. Teachers dropped their cloaks of seriousness, and the chatter in the classrooms and hallways felt like a sports bus after a big win. Even bitter enemies seemed to be under a flag of truce, but after sixth period Jalen was surprised when he turned to find Chris blocking his way in the hall.

"Hey." Chris's sling was gone, another good sign, but he wore a menacing frown.

"Hey," Jalen said. "What's up?"

"I thought we should talk."

"Okay. Shoot." Jalen tried to keep his voice from shaking.

"Pretty funny, those rabbit turds in my lunch, huh?" Chris's frown became a bitter smile.

"I . . . have no idea." Jalen's muscles tightened from a fresh jolt of fear.

"Yeah, you do." Chris narrowed his eyes but kept his hands to himself.

"I didn't do that."

"Maybe, but you knew about it." Chris folded his long arms and leaned into the lockers, striking a casual pose. It looked to Jalen like he was holding up the wall. "But I want to bury the hatchet, you know?"

Jalen rubbed his jaw, which was still sore, if not swollen.

"I mean, we're on the same team, right?" Chris raised his eyebrows.

"Where is this coming from?" Jalen looked around. Maybe someone was videotaping his response. Maybe someone was about to spill a can of paint over his head.

Chris shrugged. "I'm just a good guy."

Jalen snorted.

"No?" Chris looked offended.

"Maybe." Jalen looked around. The hallways were beginning to empty. He took a step backward. "I don't know."

"You should know." Chris unfolded his arms and stepped forward. "If I wasn't a good guy, I'd be beating the *crap* out of you right now."

"It wasn't me. I swear."

"Yeah, well, if I were you, I'd just quit right now."

"Quit?"

"The Rockets." Chris folded his arms again. "Just quit. Again, here I am being the nice guy, because you are not going to want to go through everything I've got planned for you this summer. But I was thinking, instead of being distracted by the punishment I need to inflict on you and your scurvy friend, I'd rather focus on my curveball. But if you're around . . . well, I can't let you get away with what you did."

"You can't scare me." Jalen straightened his back.

"No?" Chris smiled and nodded and turned to walk away.

The instant Jalen relaxed, Chris spun around, shrieked like a demon, and lunged right at him.

36

CHRIS STOPPED JUST SHORT OF SMASHING INTO
Jalen, as if he were some crazed guard dog on a chain.

His bared teeth nearly touched Jalen's nose.

Jalen blinked at the puff of rotten breath. He felt like he'd nearly peed his pants, and he knew his face must have been the picture of shock and fear, because Chris laughed loud and hard, pointing at Jalen as he walked away backward down the hall.

Jalen took a deep breath and gathered his wits. The bell rang. He was late.

Fortunately, the easy mood of the last day kept his teacher from saying anything as he slipped into his seat in math class. The teacher, Ms. Smythe, handed out a sheet with ten problems on it and returned to her desk, holding up her own copy.

"Just for fun, I thought I'd give you ten questions you might see on the ACT test in high school. I know it's a long way off, but we actually worked on these concepts during the year and I think with some effort, some of you will be able to solve these."

"Are we getting graded?" someone asked.

Ms. Smythe smiled. "No, it's just for fun, to test yourself and realize what's up ahead in math. Try them. You'll see. Oh, and I did include one question that you won't know just as a teaser. Anyone who gives me five correct answers gets a coupon for a free pizza at Pavone's Pizza in town."

That got everyone's attention, and all of a sudden the annoyance turned into a fun challenge. Everyone loved Pavone's pizzas.

Jalen looked at the paper and was so distracted by what Chris had said that he jotted down the answers to every single one, set his pencil down, and delivered his sheet to Ms. Smythe's desk.

She looked up and lowered her glasses, surprised and disappointed. "Jalen, you're one of my better students. I was hoping you'd really try on this. . . ."

"I . . ." Jalen looked around the room. Everyone was staring at him. He felt his face grow warm, and he returned to his seat, where he secretly took out his new iPhone. He hid it beneath the edge of his desk and began to read up on the stats from the previous night's MLB games. Lost in the numbers, Jalen didn't realize that the voice calling out in the back of his mind was his teacher's until—when he finally looked up—everyone was staring at him again.

Ms. Smythe was holding up his sheet. "Jalen? I said, did you guess on these?"

"I . . . yes." Jalen felt suddenly damp under his arms.

"No." Ms. Smythe shook her head. "I don't believe you did. You got every one of these correct, and the odds of that are more than a million to one."

"Actually, one in ten million two hundred forty thousand," Jalen said before he could stop himself. The number had simply popped into his head before he could realize he shouldn't be saying it, because it only confirmed for his teacher what was really going on in his brain.

A couple of kids laughed nervously. Ms. Smythe frowned and shook her head before adjusting her glasses and returning her attention to the paperwork on her desk. Everyone else went back to their handout—eager for a free pizza—and Jalen tried to focus on his stats, even though his brain kept trying to come up with the solution to the unsolvable problem of finding an excuse for how he'd answered everything correctly and so fast.

Before the bell finally rang, Ms. Smythe called for the worksheets to be turned in. Many of Jalen's classmates groaned because they'd only completed half the questions. Ms. Smythe quickly graded the papers and announced that only Jalen had won a pizza.

"I'm glad you all tried, though," she said, just as the bell rang.

As the room emptied out, Jalen wasn't surprised to feel Ms. Smythe's hand on his shoulder. "You and I need to talk, okay?"

37

JALEN REMAINED BEHIND AS THE CLASSROOM emptied.

"You want your free pizza, right?" Ms. Smythe handed him the coupon.

"Thank you."

"You're welcome. Now, will you tell me why you're hiding your ability?" she asked. "Why have you hidden it all year? You're not a B-plus math student. You're gifted."

Jalen looked down at his sneakers and told the truth. "I don't want to do math. I want to be a professional baseball player."

Ms. Smythe frowned. "Why can't you do both? Play ball and become a mathematician?"

Jalen shrugged. "I don't want to be a freak."

She huffed. "How does being a brilliant math student make you a freak?"

Jalen looked up. He saw the excitement in her eyes. He'd seen that before, in fourth grade when Mrs. Boehr started having him tested: pulled out of class and sitting in an empty room with strangers asking him questions, writing them out on a dry-erase board for him to solve, and talking about Jalen going to a special school his dad could never afford. "I better go, so I'm not late for my next class."

Ms. Smythe put her hand on his arm and gave it a squeeze. "You can always let me know if you change your mind. I can help you, Jalen. You have no idea how the world could open up for you."

"Thank you, Ms. Smythe. Have a nice summer." Jalen got out of there fast. If he could have kicked himself in the backside, he would have. He didn't want to stand out that way, as a math whiz.

After his last class, Jalen joined the stampede of kids rushing out the main entrance of the school. There were cheers and laughter, and the sun shone down on them all, promising the joy of summer to come. The bus ride was a circus. The air was filled with delighted howls and flying things like spitballs, erasers, and worn-down pencil nubs.

In the mayhem, Jalen told Daniel about his meeting with Chris in the hallway before seventh period.

"He can't scare us." Daniel raised a defiant chin.

"He scared me, to be honest," Jalen said.

"Yeah, but he's not going to scare you off, right?"

"I guess not."

"No, he's not." Daniel shook his head. "Hey, the Yankees started at 1:05, right? What's the score? How's JY doing?"

Jalen forgot that he could now check these things on his new phone. He fished it out of his pocket and went to his ESPN app. "He's 0-for-3 right now, but the Yankees are winning 4–1."

"Nice." Daniel slapped him a high five. "Too bad Cat's not here. I swear, it's so weird. Her stepfather barely knows she's alive, the girl gets no spending money at all, but he makes her ride to and from school with a driver."

"It's not a tough problem for her to have," Jalen said.

"It's silly is all. Like she's gonna catch something from us."

"Well," Jalen said, "you know Cat doesn't think that way."

At Jalen's stop in the center of town, Daniel said, "Pick you up at five thirty."

Later that afternoon, when they rolled into the parking lot beside the baseball field, Jalen thanked Daniel's mom, then turned to assess his team. Nothing looked unusual. A handful of players were already there tossing baseballs back and forth. Others were arriving in their own cars. The two coaches stood by home plate, talking.

When Coach Gamble called them in, the team knelt in a two-row semicircle, ready for their instructions for afternoon practice.

The coach pointed at Jalen and Daniel. "You two—run around the field until I tell you to stop."

"Why?" Daniel demanded.

"Why?" Coach Gamble wrinkled his forehead in disbelief. "Because I said so, that's why."

"You can't just punish us for no reason." Daniel raised his chin and remained on his knee like the other players around him.

"You want a reason?" Coach Gamble glared.

"Yes."

"Think about it," the coach snarled. "Think about a reason I might need to punish you two clowns. How about not knowing how to be a good teammate? Does that ring a bell in your thick skull?"

"How many laps?" Daniel asked.

Jalen wanted to tell him to just stop talking, to get up and get going and get it over with, but Daniel had fire burning in his eyes.

"I said you'll run until I tell you to stop!"

"Are Chris and Dirk and Caleb running with us?" Daniel asked, apparently unmoved by his coach's rage. "Because if you are handing out punishments for people who aren't good teammates, then you have to remember the beanballs and trashing the sandwiches someone's dad made too."

"You don't seem to understand, Bellone." Coach Gamble clenched his teeth. "*I'm* the coach here. I call the shots. Now you can either start running until you puke or you can march right off this field, because if you say another smart-mouthed word to me, if you do *anything* but start running, you're finished with the Rockets."

No one made a sound.

All eyes were on Daniel.

Daniel stood up and dusted the dirt off his knees. "Then I guess I'm finished."

He spun around and walked away from the team.

Everyone now turned to Jalen, who was frozen in place, thinking about everything he'd done to be a part of this travel team, the time, the effort, and the money it had cost.

How could he give that up?

38

DANIEL STOPPED HALFWAY TO THE DUGOUT AND
called, "Jalen, you coming?"

"You bet!" Jalen shouted, standing and moving toward
his friend. With every step after the first, he felt lighter and
lighter. He remembered that the Bronxville Bandits were
out there, and he began to smile. By the time he reached
Daniel, he was practically floating. They slapped a high five
and laughed together as they gathered up their gear.

The Rockets began their practice as if nothing had
happened. The shrill spurts of Coach Gamble's whistle
seemed silly and small as Jalen zipped up his bag, and he
wondered how he ever could have let that sound or Coach
Gamble's growling face upset him. They shouldered their

bags and left by the back of the dugout. When they hit the parking lot, Jalen skipped a few steps and spun around, walking backward.

"I can't believe we just did that," he said.

Daniel grinned, marching along. "That was absolute hot sauce—making us run? But they can't take your dignity unless you surrender it. Someone famous said something like that, I think. I don't know, maybe I made it up."

As they slogged back toward the center of town, they chattered on about the looks on everyone's faces and how bad the Rockets were going to be without them.

"Wait till they see us this weekend in our Bronxville uniforms!" Daniel laughed. "I can't wait for that."

"Wait, what?" Jalen said. The thought of Bronxville had been in his mind as well. The instant before he walked, he recalled Coach Allen's plea for him to join the team. He hadn't wanted to before, because it felt wrong to leave Daniel to fend for himself with the Rockets. But when Daniel pulled the plug on his own, it seemed to Jalen that he'd be free to join the Bandits without being disloyal. Of course, he still *wanted* Daniel to join too. He hoped Daniel *could* join, and Jalen would do anything in his power to see it happen. Yet at the same, he now felt free to play for Coach Allen whether Daniel was with him or not.

"Yeah, Bronxville." Daniel narrowed his eyes and

looked ahead before glancing at Jalen. "I know you said the coach wasn't all that excited about having us on the Bandits, but that's all we've got now, so we'll have to make the best of it."

"Uh, I don't know if he *will* take us."

Daniel stopped in his tracks. "Wait, you said he wasn't as excited about it as you thought he'd be. You never said he might not take you. Or take us."

"We never really talked about it," Jalen said.

"Talked about it? I thought we were set." Daniel's face sank.

Jalen swallowed and looked back in the direction of the park. "You mean, you did that because you thought we could just join Bronxville?"

"Join them and whip these idiots in the Boston tournament. Yes." Daniel suddenly wore a look of panic. "I was thinking we had a place to go! What are we going to do all summer? Catch frogs?"

Daniel began to pace back and forth on the sidewalk. He grabbed the thick dark hair sticking out on either side of his cap and pulled with both hands until his cap tumbled to the ground. "Oh my God. Oh my God."

Jalen felt guilty. He knew how Daniel felt, because *he* wouldn't have walked away either if the likelihood of playing for Bronxville hadn't been a possibility his mind.

He put a hand on Daniel's shoulder. "Okay, don't go nuts on me."

"Nuts?" Daniel had a wild look in his eyes. "I'm not going nuts. I'm going to go whacked-out, loony-bin, out-of-my-mind crazy if I can't get on that team. And what about our money? My parents paid a thousand dollars for me to be on the Rockets. I didn't even think about the money."

Daniel plunked down right there in the grass beside the sidewalk and put his face into his hands. A man cutting his lawn across the street paused to look at them for a moment before continuing his work.

Jalen sat down beside Daniel and gently grabbed him by the back of the neck. "Hey, come on, it's gonna be okay."

"It is? How can you say that?" Daniel looked up with wide eyes. "Do you have a plan? Tell me you do."

"Okay," said Jalen. "I have a plan."

39

CAT MET THEM AT THE GATES OF MOUNT TIPTON.

Daniel had used Jalen's phone to let his parents know that they didn't need a ride home from practice. "Cat's picking us up," he'd said, explaining to Jalen that it was sort of true. They left their gear bags in the bushes and headed next door to JY's mansion—an enormous home built on its own hill and surrounded by its own gates and wall, but nowhere near as big as Cat's place. The gates were open and they marched up the driveway, past the bronze fountain and its angels struggling for a trumpet that sprayed a geyser of water, and right up to the front door.

Cat rang the bell and JY's two Rottweilers, Butch and Missy, went bananas inside.

"Doesn't he know we're coming?" Daniel's eyes got wide at the sound of the dogs.

"I told him." Cat pointed at the Ferrari parked in the circle. "And he's back."

"Maybe he just forgot his dogs want to eat my leg," Daniel said.

The dogs continued to bark.

Cat took out her phone and sent a text. They stood staring at one another. Cat checked her phone.

Daniel said, "I wonder if *Guinness World Records* has a page for the longest a dog ever barked without stopping."

Cat's phone dinged and she read the text. "He's out back. At the cage. Come on."

They tramped around the house, following a brick path that took them to some steps and down past the pool area. The white light from the batting cage was brighter than the twilight. The whir of the pitching machine was interrupted every few seconds by the thunk of a pitch and the crack of the bat on the ball. Deep inside the heavy web of netting, the bat flashed with each stroke. JY was going at it with the steady rhythm of a farm machine.

Cat burst right through the slit in the netting. "Hey."

JY rested his bat, letting it hang from one hand without turning off the machine. He looked awful. His eyes were red and sagging, and he needed a shave.

"Hey." He wore a baggy pair of sweatpants and a ragged T-shirt that crept to the edges of his lean biceps. "So, Foxx is having a field day with this. He won't even return my agent's calls. It's like he knows I'm melting down."

He took a deep breath and let it out as if waiting for Cat to speak.

"So, we're here," she said.

JY nodded and addressed Jalen. "Can you make it to the game tomorrow night?"

Jalen swallowed a lump in his throat. "That depends."

"Of course it does." JY's hair looked matted from a nap on the plane ride home, and his shiny white smile bloomed like a lie in the middle of his tired face. "I have to strike a deal with your agent here, I know that, but let's say I do, can you be there?"

"I don't care about the money," Jalen said.

"I do." Cat slapped his arm to be quiet. "I'm handling that. We agreed."

"I don't know where I'll be tomorrow night is all," Jalen said.

JY pointed the bat at Jalen. "Because aliens might abduct you? What are you talking about?"

"Let's talk dollars." Cat turned to Jalen. "Will you please let me do my job?"

"Okay," Jalen said.

"Great." JY spun around, stepped on the pedal that released a pitch, and drilled it into the netting before turning back. "Now we'll cut a deal that might not even happen. Okay, let's get this over with. You're at five thousand, and I'm at five hundred. Let's make a deal."

"My last offer was nine thousand five hundred," Cat said. "I never said five. You said five."

JY turned and blasted another pitch before answering. "That was halfway between my five hundred and your ten thousand. I was trying to save time, as I'd like to do now so I can hit three dozen more balls and then get some sleep."

"Are you offering five thousand?" Cat raised an eyebrow.

JY gritted his teeth. "Yes. I am."

"Now, here's where I would normally say to make it seventy-five hundred and we've got a deal."

Jalen winced at the smoking-mad look on JY's face, but Cat seemed unfazed. "But I'm not saying that because we're all friends, right?"

"I thought so," said JY.

"Yes, we are," Cat said, "and that's why we can work with your number if you're willing to help us out a bit with some other things?"

"More tweets?" JY raised an eyebrow.

"Yes, but something else, too." Cat held up her hands. "Nothing terribly difficult, just a light lift for you."

"Okay, well, you need to tell me what," JY said. Before Cat could reply, Jalen said, "Help with the Bronxville Bandits."

40

"IT'S NOT THAT BIG OF A DEAL," JALEN SAID AFTER explaining what he wanted JY to do.

"Oh, no?" JY turned and whacked a few more pitches as he spoke. "You just said the Bandits only had one spot. How do I fix that? Am I supposed to take out some kid's knees with this bat?"

Daniel looked horrified, and he muttered, "Hot sauce."

"You're James Yager," Cat interrupted. "The rules don't apply."

JY laughed.

"They don't," Cat insisted. "Look how you got the Silver Liner fixed up in four days. No one else could do that, but *you* did. What are you known for in baseball?"

"I don't know," he said. "Batting a thousand, I guess."

"Before all this," Cat said.

"Double play, I guess."

"That's right," Cat said, "the double play. That time Jeter fed you some mustard and you caught it with your bare hand so you could chuck it to first on that double play against the Red Sox. That's you. You get two outs when the normal person—even the normal MLB player—gets just one."

"Okay, so let's say I buy what you're selling," JY said. "I *try* to get the coach to take you guys, but he's not as impressed with me as you are. Do we still have a deal for five thousand a game?"

"You gotta try your hardest," Jalen said.

"And if I do, and it still doesn't work, I want to know if we have a deal."

"Yes," Jalen said. "Of course."

"Good." JY turned and hit another pitch. "'Cause I'd like to get some help tomorrow night."

"Would you mind if I just asked you for one more thing?" The deal was going so well that Jalen had to give his other idea a try. "Please?"

"Seriously?" JY scowled at Cat like it was her fault. She shrugged.

"I want you to tell people what I can do," Jalen said. "I'd like people to know."

"Why?" JY asked. "Why do you *need* people to know? 'Cause I gotta tell you, *that* could be a deal breaker for me."

41

JALEN LOOKED AT HIS FRIENDS.

Even though they knew his secret, he felt funny saying it aloud in front of them and JY at the same time.

He clenched his hands. "I want to find my mom."

"Your mom?" JY blinked and rubbed the scruff on his chin. "What's that got to do with telling everyone you're a baseball genius?"

"If she sees me on TV or something, reads about me, maybe she'll come back." Jalen felt entirely stupid. "I don't mean come back, like, to live with us, but I could at least meet her. See her. If she knew I was kind of famous—and I'm pretty sure that's what would happen if people knew what I was doing—then I think I'd have a chance."

"Do you know where she is?" JY asked. "Any idea at all?"

Jalen looked at his shoes. "No."

"But you know her name, right?" JY asked.

"Yes. Elizabeth Johnson."

"Good." JY tapped his bat on the concrete to get Jalen's attention. "Look, your mom's not gonna care if you're famous. That's not what's going on—I'm not sure what *is* going on, but you being famous isn't the answer."

"Then what is?" Cat asked, and Jalen felt grateful to her.

"You *find* her," JY said. "She probably feels bad after all these years. She's probably waiting for you to reach out to her, and you don't need to be famous for that either."

"Then how?" Jalen asked.

"Private detective." JY pointed the barrel of his bat at Jalen. "You hire someone good with all that money I'll be paying you. He tracks her down and lets her know you'd like to see her. I bet she'll be thrilled."

"I thought about a private detective, but I can't afford one. And why do you think she'd be thrilled?" The question escaped Jalen without thought.

"Because . . ." JY gave him a funny look. "Don't you know? You're . . . you're a great kid, Jalen. You're special. Anyone would be proud to have you as their son."

Jalen felt the blush on his cheeks, and he looked down again.

"The only question is how much you're willing to spend," JY said. "It might be an easy thing for a good detective to do, or it could take time and cost thousands. You never know."

"I'd spend it all," Jalen said. "Everything except what it costs us to join the Bandits."

"I don't know if I can take money from you like that, Jalen," Daniel said.

"You're part of this, Daniel. You've helped me all along the way, and you deserve it."

"That's if Coach Allen even lets us join," Daniel said.

Cat spoke up. "When James Yager asks, James Yager receives."

"I'll try," JY said. "So long as we go the detective route instead of the famous route. That okay with you, Jalen?"

"It's a deal." Jalen held out a hand, and JY shook it.

42

A QUICK CHECK OF HIS FACEBOOK PAGE SHOWED that by day Coach Allen was an accountant at a private firm in White Plains. Nights and weekends, he was the Bandits' head coach. JY told Jalen that the right way to get what they wanted was to meet in person, over lunch.

"If this is going to work," JY said the next morning before calling Coach Allen's cell phone, "we're going to have to turn your coach into our friend."

"Why?" Jalen asked.

"Because he's going to need to work with us. You may have to miss some practices here and there to help me out, and I want him to be on board. If he's our friend, we won't have to worry. He'll be part of the team, so to speak."

JY dialed the number and got no answer, so he left a message. "Coach? James Yager here . . . from the Yankees. I know it seems strange—getting a call from me—but I'm friends with Jalen DeLuca. He gave me your number, and I'm hoping we can sit down and talk today. We've got a game tonight, but maybe lunch? Call me."

"Great," Jalen said. "How about the detective?"

"We're all business this morning, aren't we?" JY said. "I already beat you to it. I spoke to Miles Endwell, the head of Yankees security, and he's got the perfect person for us. It's a woman he used to work with in the Secret Service. He says she's great, and he's going to text me later on when we can meet her."

"Okay, awesome . . . Now what?" Jalen asked. They sat in JY's office with Cat and Daniel.

"How about the batting cage?" JY suggested. "We can get tuned up while we're waiting for your coach to call back."

"He's not our coach yet," Daniel said.

"Yet," said JY. "Come on."

They trooped out back to the cage, where JY hit a couple of dozen balls before instructing Daniel and Jalen, letting them each hit a few dozen balls of their own.

"You're doing a good job with that shoulder," JY said, following up on some earlier instructions he'd given to

Jalen before his trip to Cleveland. "Try to open up that left foot a bit. I think that might help, but see how it feels."

It felt good, and Jalen glowed with pride as he drove the pitches into the netting.

"Wow," Cat said.

"Yeah, looking good." JY scratched his chin. "Coach Allen, watch out."

"Rockton Rockets, watch out," Daniel said.

"I thought you were done with the Rockets," JY said.

"Not with them, but *against* them." Daniel tightened the grip on his bat and took half a swing. "If we can get on the Bandits, we'll probably face them this weekend in Boston."

"There's a travel team tournament in Boston for you guys this weekend?" JY raised his eyebrows. "*We* play in Boston too."

"Maybe you can see us play?" Daniel said.

Jalen didn't join in. He didn't want to ask JY to do more than he was already doing, and he had to think the Yankees star player had more to do in Boston than show up for the 13U tournament.

"Maybe," JY said, surprising Jalen. "I'd like to see you guys in action. Let's see what the timing is like. We play Friday night, then Saturday afternoon, and Sunday evening, so . . ."

Jalen realized JY was staring at him. Daniel was too.

Jalen rested his bat on the concrete. "What?"

JY licked his lips. "Man, could I use you against David Price."

"Yes!" Daniel pumped his fist. "Jalen helps you, and you come watch us play. I love that."

"My mom and I could take a road trip and help coordinate everything," Cat said. "I've never been to Fenway."

Jalen felt a surge of excitement too. Helping his Yankees beat their archrivals at the Green Monster? Plus, anything that would make JY work harder to convince Coach Allen to find a spot for them on the Bandits was a good thing, a great thing.

"Sure," Jalen said. "We should be able to work something out, especially if Cat's mom is there to help out. That's *if* we're in Boston with the Bandits."

As if on cue, JY's phone rang.

He looked at the number of the incoming call, smiled, and said, "Well, we're about to find out."

43

JY MADE SOME SMALL TALK WITH COACH ALLEN
about the Yankees season and the Bronxville team. He
paused to listen before saying, "Yes, I am calling you about
Jalen."

He listened again and said, "It's really something I need
to discuss in person, if you don't mind. . . ."

Jalen crossed his fingers and looked at Cat. She winked
at him, confident.

"Great," JY said. "How about the Ritz-Carlton in White
Plains at noon? I'll get a private room."

Jalen and Cat slapped high fives with each other and
then with Daniel.

"And, Coach," JY said, "can you tell me if your team is

practicing tonight? Oh, good. No, I'll explain when I see you."

The Yankees player hung up and grinned at Jalen. "Looks like you've got an appointment at Yankee Stadium tonight. The Calamari Kid is back. You all just check with your parents."

"Are we going too?" Cat asked.

"I already got four seats set aside," JY said. "Right there behind the on-deck circle. If it ain't broke, don't fix it, right?"

"Wow." Daniel snapped his fingers. "We were so close last time I could tell what cologne Gardner had on."

"That's kind of weird," Cat said in a pleasant tone.

"You're weird," Daniel said.

"Takes one to know one," Cat replied.

"Who's on the mound tonight for Houston?" Jalen asked.

"McCullers is supposed to start," JY said.

All the numbers the young Astros pitcher had put up over the past couple of seasons popped into Jalen's mind without effort. "Really a two-pitch guy, four-seam and a breaker, but he will throw the changeup—two years ago in his playoff game against the Royals, he threw it twelve percent of the time."

Cat and Daniel looked at each other with open mouths.

JY chuckled and shook his head. "This is why I love stuffed calamari at the Silver Liner."

They made their phone calls and hit some more balls before they cleaned up and climbed into JY's Mercedes SUV, a black G55, with room for them all to stretch out on the trip to White Plains. When they pulled up to the hotel entrance, the doorman and valets instantly recognized JY. They straightened themselves and greeted him in hushed and somber voices.

"Good morning, Mr. Yager."

"Welcome, Mr. Yager."

"Do you need anything, Mr. Yager?"

Daniel popped the wad of gum he'd been chewing out of his mouth and turned to the doorman in his scarlet uniform and gold-braided cap. "Have you got a place I can put this?"

"Of course." Without hesitation, the doorman handed him a tissue, which he then threw away.

Doors opened, and people stopped to stare as the little group, led by the famous baseball player, marched through the lobby, where more wide-eyed people wanted to know what they could do for James Yager.

Jalen ached to be like JY one day, not just an MLB player, but a *famous* player, one who everyone recognized and liked and wanted to be near, especially the mother who'd left him behind.

They went to the top floor and were seated at a round table in the corner of a grand suite by the windows. Waiters fluttered around the table like birds at a feeder, bringing water and bread, or just to steal a glimpse at James Yager. JY either didn't notice or pretended not to. Jalen didn't think he could ever grow used to, or tired of, the kind of special attention people gave to JY.

Coach Allen appeared, wearing a suit and tie and with his short gray hair slicked down and parted on the side. He looked taller and thinner than Jalen remembered. As he was escorted through the suite toward their table, Jalen saw that the coach hadn't expected that three kids would be joining him and JY for lunch.

The two men shook hands, and then JY introduced Coach Allen to Cat and Daniel before saying, "And I know you've already met Jalen."

Coach Allen nodded and sat down. They ordered right away because JY told the head waiter that he had to get to the stadium. Jalen and his friends sat quietly and watched as JY charmed the coach. The two of them talked a lot of baseball, and JY showed a special interest in Coach Allen's baseball experience, which included four years on the Siena College team. Their food came, and Jalen sank his teeth into a hot pastrami sandwich. As the conversation between JY and Coach Allen dragged on, Jalen began to worry about why it was taking JY so long to get down to business, but Cat—who kept her eyes glued to the two men—seemed happy, and that gave him some comfort. Trying to be calm, he tackled the french fries.

Finally JY leaned forward and lowered his voice. "Dave, I need your help with something."

Coach Allen blinked and sat up straight. "Of course. What can I do?"

"First of all," JY said, "this is completely confidential. You have to promise you'll keep this between us."

Coach Allen studied the Yankees second baseman for a minute before he nodded. "Okay, I can promise that."

"Good. So, Jalen and Daniel and Cat, they've been help-ing me." JY nodded toward the three friends. "With my batting slump. I know it's gonna sound strange—I can't believe it myself sometimes—but Jalen can predict the kind of ball a pitcher is about to throw. He really can. . . ."

Both men looked at Jalen, and he tried to meet their gazes with a look of confidence, even though that wasn't how he felt.

Coach Allen wore a crooked smile, and he looked around as if someone might be filming the scene before he turned to JY. "So, you're kidding me here, right? I don't get it."

"No." JY shook his head once. "I'm not kidding. I'm being serious, and I need your help now too."

"He knows *every* pitch?" Coach Allen asked, obviously confused.

"Yeah," JY said, "just about. It took me a bit to accept it too. It's kind of unreal. Then I had him show Derek Jeter. We went to his place to watch a game together, and Derek was like, 'Hey, the kid's for real. Go for it.' That's when I knew I wasn't losing my mind. The rest—as they say—is history."

"You are serious!" Coach Allen looked out the window into the distance for a few moments, considering. Then he said, "Umm, okay, what do you need me to do?"

Jalen grinned at his friends and let go a deep breath he hadn't even realized he'd been holding.

JY put a hand on the coach's shoulder. "I need you to let these guys play on your team, and I may need some help with Jalen missing a practice here or there if I have to have him help me at the stadium."

"Oh, gosh. I see." Coach Allen's face turned red. "Look, I'd *really* love to do that for you . . . but I can't."

44

JY'S HAND SLIPPED OFF THE COACH'S SHOULDER.

"You can't?" He tilted his head as if he'd heard wrong.

"We only have room for sixteen players," Coach Allen said. "When Jalen told me no-go, I offered the spot to another kid."

"Did he take it?" JY asked.

"Not yet, but that's just one spot. Even if he says no, I can't take them both. It was a big deal when I expanded the roster from fourteen to sixteen. These baseball parents are tough. Everyone wants their kid to get playing time, so the roster limit is set. I can't go back on my word." Coach Allen looked like he *wanted* to take both Jalen and Daniel.

JY pursed his lips and puffed out his cheeks.

"What about this?" Cat's voice took everyone but Jalen by surprise. Nothing about a girl who wanted to be president, a talk-show host, or a sports agent could surprise him anymore.

"What if," Cat continued, "you take them both for practice, and you rotate them for the games? Then, if someone else gets hurt or they have a family obligation, you've got a player in reserve."

"I couldn't rotate them in and out." Coach Allen frowned at his silverware and flipped the fork on its edge before looking up. "Having an extra player around will make some parents upset, but I can weather that storm. Best I can do is have Daniel practice with us, and, if someone gets hurt for the season, he can take the spot, but no guarantees. What about the fee? Who's going to cover that?"

"How much?" JY asked.

"Fifteen hundred," said the coach. "Each."

"I got that covered." JY looked at Cat. "An advance."

Cat turned her attention on their friend. "Daniel?"

Daniel looked around at them all with his mouth open, but no words coming out.

"It's not a bad offer," JY said.

"We can't go back to the Rockets anyway, Daniel," Jalen said. "And you don't have to worry about the fee."

Daniel chewed on his lower lip, then said, "Okay. I'm in."

"Yes!" Cat high-fived Jalen before she froze, then turned toward Coach Allen. "Oh. I forgot. One more thing."

Coach Allen raised his eyebrows. "And that is?"

"Could I do stats for the games?" Cat wore a winning smile. "I know a lot about baseball, and I'm easy to get along with."

Daniel barked a laugh. "Like a cobra."

Cat gave him a melting look.

"The tame kind." Daniel forced a smile. "Like with the guy in a turban, swaying back and forth, so calming."

Under his breath Daniel said, "Just watch out for her bite."

"What'd you say?" Cat glared at him.

Daniel's face filled with panic. "Just how you're always *right*."

Coach Allen looked at JY, who shrugged. "In my experience, things seem to go better when you give this young lady what she wants."

"Uh, sure," the coach said. "I don't see why not."

"That's great, Coach." Cat patted Jalen's shoulder. "You just got yourself a baseball genius."

"Super. Then I'll text my other recruit and tell him we're full." Coach Allen took out his phone.

Jalen picked a string of pastrami from his teeth before

Cat signaled that he also had a spot of Russian dressing on his cheek. Coach Allen got Cat's and Jalen's phone numbers to put them on his team texts.

"Don't forget Daniel," Cat said.

"You manage him too?" Coach Allen asked.

"Yeah. He's like a brother," she said, causing Daniel to blush as he gave his number.

They left the hotel, and JY dropped Cat and Daniel at the mall where they were meeting Cat's mom. She was going to take them home before heading back to the game that evening. It was just Jalen and JY in the SUV. Before hitting the road, JY read a text on his phone and said, "So the detective who's gonna find your mom is meeting us at the stadium."

"Right now?" Jalen felt a current of excitement buzz through his body.

"Yup," JY said. "Right now."

45

IT WASN'T THE FIRST TIME JALEN HAD PULLED
past the guard and down into the players' underground
parking garage, but it was still a thrill. All the shiny new
rides packed in together reminded Jalen of a box of fancy
chocolates, each one different, but delicious-looking, so
that you couldn't help wanting them all. They got out and
headed toward the clubhouse. Jalen recognized an olive-
green Bentley convertible, a red Ferrari, a black Lincoln
Navigator decked out in chrome, and a deep blue Tesla
Roadster.

JY held the door for Jalen, and they walked down a
long corridor, past the clubhouse entrance, until they
came to Miles Endwell's office. The security director had

his assistant bring them into a meeting room. A red-haired woman in jeans and a Patagonia pullover shell with a Timberland cap pulled low on her head sat chewing gum and talking on her phone. When she saw them, she held up a finger, quickly finished her call, and stood to greet them.

"Hi, I'm Emery Moore." Her face was spotted with freckles, and her bright green eyes were sharp.

They shook her hand and sat down across the table.

Emery clasped her hands and rested them on the table. "So, you'd like me to find your mom?"

Jalen's mouth sagged open. It was a big moment. "Uhh, yes."

"That's what I do, so . . ." Emery looked at JY. "And you're good with my rates?"

"Yes." JY turned to Jalen. "I gave her a ten-thousand-dollar retainer to start. Your first two games for me."

"Plus the travel team fees." Jalen felt uncomfortable owing JY thirteen thousand dollars, but without the detective he'd be nowhere.

"It'll all work out." JY waved a hand in the air. "So, Emery, Miles says you're the best."

"Yeah, I'd say that's right." She chewed her gum and took out a pad of paper and a pen. She pointed the pen at Jalen. "So, tell me everything you know about her. JY told me her name, but there are way too many Elizabeth

Johnsons to go through. I'll need as many details as you can give me."

JY and Emery stared at Jalen. His brain seemed to collapse in on itself the way a sand castle crumbles under a thick ocean wave. He felt his face catch fire.

JY cleared his throat and tried to help. "She was pretty young. Right, Jalen?"

"Yes." Jalen looked at his hands, their skin the color of coffee with milk, brown and white together. "I think she was a singer."

"Professionally?" Emery asked.

"Uh-huh."

"That's good. Any pictures?"

"One." Jalen looked up.

"Great. Can you get that for me?"

"Uh . . ." It was all he had of his mom.

"Just take a picture with your phone and text it to me." Emery snapped her gum. "I don't need the original. How about her birthplace? Where she went to school? Anything like that?"

"I don't think so," Jalen said, "but I can ask."

"How about her family?"

"No."

"JY told me she and your dad got married."

"So he could get his green card and stay," Jalen said.

DOUBLE PLAY

"That's good." Emery wrote that down. "See if you can find out where they got married. I can get a copy of the license, and that will tell me a lot."

"It will?" JY asked.

"Sure, it'll have her parents' names and addresses. That'll be money."

Jalen realized his heart was pounding frantically, as if trying to escape his chest. "So, you think you can find her?"

"Me?" Emery laughed and pointed a thumb into her chest. "Last person I had to find disappeared from a church mission in Paraguay. That was a challenge, and I still got her. This is a Rubik's Cube with two sides already done. Yeah, I'll find her."

Jalen looked at JY. He was afraid he might cry, so he looked away and sniffed.

"The big question is, what do I do when I find her?" Emery said.

"What do you mean?" Jalen asked.

Emery glanced at JY. "No one talked to him about this?"

"Wait," Jalen said, suddenly sick to his stomach, "talked to me about what?"

197

46

THE DETECTIVE FROWNED AT JY. "REALLY? I'M
not a psychologist, you know. I find people."

"I'm a baseball player," JY said. "I don't know what to
say to him."

"Say what?" Jalen almost shouted. "Just tell me."

Emery took a deep breath and let it out with a hiss. "Sometimes these things . . . they don't . . . they can go bad on you."

"Bad?" Jalen swallowed.

"It's just that sometimes people leave one life behind
for another, and they don't appreciate being reminded of
it." Emery spoke gently. "They've blocked it out."

"But I'm sure there are a lot of times people are happy
to be found," JY said.

Emery nodded. "Yes, for sure. They love it. Sometimes they feel like they don't deserve to reach out themselves because they left, and they're thrilled that someone cared enough to find them."

"That's probably like most of the time, right?" JY said.

"Uh, no," Emery replied. "It's about fifty-fifty."

"Fifty-fifty?" Some bile crept up Jalen's throat from his stomach. He swallowed it back down.

JY flashed Emery a scowl, then said to Jalen, "But that's not your mom. She'll be excited to hear from you. Right, Emery?"

"Look," she said, addressing JY, "I know you're a famous ballplayer, and everyone wants to make you happy, but when it comes to family members, it would be crazy for me to say that it couldn't go wrong, because it can."

Emery looked at Jalen. Her face softened. "I'm sorry, but that's the truth."

Jalen sighed. "That's okay. I understand. I still want to find her."

"So the question is, once I find her, do you want me to reach out to her and tell her about you? Or would you like to be the one to make the call?" Emery pointed her pen at herself, then at Jalen. "Or do you want to ambush her? Which I never recommend, but some people insist on doing that."

Jalen thought for a moment. "If you find her and could just tell her about me . . . you know, that I'm a pretty good kid and a baseball player and that JY and I are friends and I'm helping him, and that I'd really like to just meet her . . . I think that would be good."

"I'd say he's a great kid," JY said. "And I'd also have to say he's not just helping me. He saved my career."

Pride swelled in Jalen's chest.

JY looked at his watch. "Unless there's anything else, we better get going. I need to loosen up my swing."

"No, that's about it." Emery stood up and shook JY's hand before turning to Jalen. "Do you have a phone?"

Jalen removed the iPhone from his pocket and showed her. "Yes, I do."

"Great. Give me your number, and I'll text you my contact info. See if you can find out where your parents were married and also send that picture of your mom. Get me those two things, and I should have something for you soon."

Jalen gave her his number before he said, "Soon like a couple of months?"

"I don't know," she said. "Could be months, could be weeks, could even be days. Every one of these things is different, but if she is still alive, I will find her."

"Alive?" Jalen felt his stomach shrink.

Emery put a hand on Jalen's shoulder. "She's been gone what? Eight, nine years, JY said? I'm sure she's probably fine, but you have to be ready for the worst in case it happens."

She gave his shoulder a squeeze, then walked out the door.

"So," JY said, "do you want to hang out in the players' lounge, or do you want to head out to the dugout with me?"

"I can go with you?"

JY laughed. "Yeah, you can do whatever you want. You're good luck. You're the Calamari Kid, right? Hey, what's wrong?"

"Just what she said about the worst-case scenario. I never even thought that something could have happened to my mom like that, but I guess it's possible."

JY waved his hand in the air and then opened the door for them to go. "Aw, don't worry about that. She's just got to be careful not to promise too much. I'm sure everything will work out just the way you expect it to."

JY led him out of the security offices, down the hall, and into the Yankees locker room, where the players were changing into their uniforms for batting practice. JY motioned Jalen to the big black swivel chair in front of his locker while he changed. Only once he had tied up his cleats did he look at Jalen again. "Hey, why the long face?"

"Because of what you said."

JY scrunched up his face. "About her having to say that stuff?"

"No," Jalen said, "about things turning out the way I expect them to. Lots of things haven't worked out the way I expected them to."

"You gotta be positive, Jalen. Keep your head up." The star player snugged the Yankees cap down on his head. "Doors open all the time in life. If you've got your head down, you might miss that one door that opens up on your dream."

Jalen nodded and followed JY out through the locker room doors, down the tunnel, and up the steps into the dugout.

When Jalen saw who was waiting for him, he wished he hadn't listened to JY.

He wished he'd kept his head down.

47

JEFFREY FOXX WORE A LIGHT BLUE SUIT WITH A
pink bow tie and a mean smile. Jalen squirmed under
the GM's frown. He blinked in the sunshine. The smack of
a baseball being knocked out of the park echoed off the
stands. Batting practice was in full swing.

"I know you're an old pro." Foxx stood blocking their
path. "And this place is like your second home, but toting
this kid all around like a lunch pail is a little much, don't
you think?"

"Well, you know what they say, 'Don't sweat the small
stuff.'" JY spoke in a lighthearted manner. "Especially
when there are real issues to deal with. Like, where's my
new contract, Jeffrey?"

"You fell apart in Cleveland, JY," Foxx said. "I'm surprised you'd bring up a new contract after that."

"Only because we had a deal," JY said. "And batting .180 isn't really falling apart, is it?"

"It doesn't merit a multimillion-dollar contract extension." The GM seemed to think that was funny. "But we're working on it."

"You're going to look mighty silly tonight, not getting my extension signed before I go four for four against McCullers," JY said.

Foxx raised his eyebrows and angled his head at Jalen. "That would be because of the lucky calamari, I suppose?"

"Lucky calamari, baseball genius, call it what you like," said JY. "Excuse us. I'm up. Come on, Jalen."

Jalen followed JY out of the dugout, past a surprised-looking Jeffrey Foxx.

"Am I allowed?" Jalen whispered, hustling to keep up.

JY chuckled. "Sure. You heard him. This place is my home."

Jalen removed his sunglasses from the brim of his hat and put them on as he followed JY out onto the field. They circled the big net cage that had been wheeled out to keep foul balls from zinging anyone. The third-base coach stood in front of the mound with a basket of baseballs. He threw a final pitch to Brett Gardner, who rocked it into the second deck in right field before making way for JY. The two players fist-bumped as they passed each other. Jalen let his fingers hang on the net and poked his nose through a hole to watch JY bat. JY's swing reminded Jalen of when his father filleted a fish, one smooth effortless motion that most people could never do. He enjoyed the sunshine, the sound of the batted balls, and the slight warm breeze. Happy not to see the GM, he relaxed even more.

When JY finished, they headed back into the clubhouse, where Jalen watched YouTube clips of McCullers pitching while an episode of *Law & Order* played on the lounge TV. JY disappeared into the training room for some treatment on his bad ankle. Jalen texted back and forth with Cat as he watched, so he knew they weren't far from the stadium. The thrill of being inside the players' clubhouse was no less than it had been his first time inside the previous week. It seemed dreamlike to look up and see the ballplayers he was used to watching on TV walking past him, or playing a game on their phones, or having snacks at one of the tables. The players laughed and joked with one another like kids at a sleepover party.

When Chase Headley walked by in a pair of gym shorts, he bumped fists with Jalen. "Hey, Calamari Kid. Give me some of that good luck, will ya?"

Headley gave Jalen's head a rub, and they both laughed.

JY finally returned, and Jalen looked up from his phone. "Victoria says they're crossing the street, so we can head up. We set on the signals?"

"Same as last time," Jalen said. "Four fingers for the fastball. Changeup is two thumbs up."

"Let's go with a *C* for the curve," JY said, making a *C* with his hand.

"And when a reliever comes in, the sinker is a thumbs-down and the slider is this." JY made a throat-cutting motion. "Splitter is a peace sign. Cutter is a pair of scissors."

"We're good." Jalen made a peace sign and some pretend scissors with his fingers before JY gave him a thumbs-up.

"Make sure you're subtle with these signals, okay?" JY scratched his jaw. "I don't want people catching on to this. We gotta keep the signals down low, and we're not going to be able to have a conversation during the game."

"Okay. Got it."

"And one more thing," JY said. "You know how sometimes it takes you a few pitches before you know what's going on?"

"Yeah," Jalen said.

"Well, if you ever don't know, don't fake it, okay?" JY scowled and shook his head. "Don't ever guess."

"I won't."

"Because that would ruin everything if I can't trust you," JY said.

"Okay."

Jalen followed JY out of the locker room and up the stairs toward the VIP lounge. They found Cat, her mom, and Daniel waiting in the hallway. Cat's mom gave JY a kiss on the cheek. Cat frowned and looked away, and Jalen couldn't help wondering about JY and Cat's mom. He'd keep his mouth shut, though, because it was a sore subject between him and Cat.

"Okay, buddy." JY turned to Jalen and slapped a high five. "We got this."

JY disappeared. Cat's mom led them all through the VIP lounge and out into the stands, where the Astros were finishing up their own batting practice. The only thing between their seats and home plate was a low padded concrete wall. If he stood up and looked sideways, Jalen could see over Daniel and the four older men sitting next to them and right into the Yankees dugout. He put on his sunglasses and took his seat.

The on-deck circle was just the other side of the wall. Jalen knew that JY had gotten the tickets from the owner's private stock. He assumed the four men next to them were friends of the owner's, and he wondered where Mr. Brenneck stood on the issue of JY's contract extension.

His only comment in the media was that the team was working on it.

It was a perfect evening for baseball, warm without being hot, with a breeze that tickled Jalen's skin and was just this side of being windy. Daniel filled out an order card for food, knowing from their prior visits that sitting in these VIP seats you could get anything you wanted for no extra charge.

"How about a burger and a smoothie?" Daniel asked.

Jalen shrugged. He wasn't hungry.

"I'll take that as a yes," Daniel said. "I can eat two if you change your mind."

The Astros retired before both teams reappeared to take the field for the national anthem. After the music, JY gave his friends a smile and a wave before jogging out to second base. CC took the mound and threw his eight warm-up pitches before the first Astros batter stepped up. CC gave up one double but held the Astros scoreless. JY was sixth in the batting order, so Jalen concentrated hard on the Astros pitcher, wanting to zero in on what he was doing. It could take Jalen anywhere from a couple of pitches to a couple dozen before he began to know what that next pitch was going to be. He had no idea why it sometimes happened faster or slower.

After a Reuben Hall single, McCullers put the next two

batters down with a steady mix of fastballs and those dev-
astating curves. By the time Tollerson struck out on a 3–2
count to end the inning, Jalen had McCullers pegged.

"I recognize that look." Cat studied Jalen's face. "You
got this, right?"

"I do," Jalen said.

Cat's mom and Daniel had both been listening for his
answer, and they nodded their approval.

JY emerged from the dugout. Before heading for second base, he gave Jalen a silent, questioning look. Jalen
rewarded him with a grin and an *okay* signal. JY's face lit
up with the knowledge that he'd know McCullers's pitches
when he got up in the next inning.

The top of the second dragged. CC got himself into some
trouble but pulled out of it with a relentless succession of
sinkers that rivaled the action of his opponent. Headley
was up for the Yankees. JY took the on-deck circle to
swing his bat, and once he even winked at Cat's mom.

Jalen focused on McCullers. He remembered the fist
bump Headley had given him in the locker room and
wished he could help the third baseman out of the 1–2 tight
spot he found himself in. Jalen knew the next pitch would
be a low inside fastball, but there was nothing he could do
about it. When it came, Headley swung and missed. The
crowd's groan turned to cheering as JY marched toward

the plate. Jalen glanced around and saw several people looking or even pointing his way. There weren't many Yankees fans who hadn't heard the story about the lucky Calamari Kid.

Cat nudged his ribs with an elbow. "JY's looking at you."

"Right. Sorry." Jalen shifted his focus to McCullers. He wanted to read his body language, and it told him clear as day that JY was going to see a nasty curveball out of the gate.

Jalen made a *C* with his hand, but the instant before he could raise it above the concrete wall for JY to see, a shadow fell across him.

Jalen blinked in confusion and realized that some enormous person had stepped out of the dugout to stand right in front of him, blocking his view of the batter.

"Hey!" The sound escaped Jalen at the same moment that he realized the man was a police officer.

As McCullers went into his windup, Jalen recognized the officer as the same one who'd taken him to Jeffrey Foxx's office. He also knew as certain as he knew the next pitch that the officer being there was no coincidence.

The giant cop Foxx had called Jimmy was intentionally blocking Jalen's signals.

48

"STRIKE!" THE UMPIRE'S CALL STRUCK A NOTE
of panic in Jalen's chest. He sat frozen by surprise and
the natural caution created by such a hulking officer.

"Hey!" Cat had no natural caution—or if she did, she
ignored it. She was up out of her seat. She seemed to
know what was going on as well, and she jabbed a finger in the huge policeman's back. "You can't stand there.
You're blocking our view."

The cop swung his head slowly around without shifting
his position. McCullers studied the sign from his catcher,
shook him off, nodded, and prepared to go into his windup.
Jalen knew it was another curve. He stood up and tried to
peer around the big blue uniformed cop, but he was too

wide. Jalen made a *C* with his hand and held it as high as he could, but he had no idea if JY had seen it as the pitcher began his windup.

"Strike!" shouted the ump.

"Please!" Cat shouted. "You're in our *way!*"

"Officer?" Cat's mom sounded stern, like a teacher chewing out a kid for throwing spitballs. "You're blocking our view."

The policeman grabbed either side of the thick black leather gun belt around his waist. He shifted it, but said nothing. It was as if he hadn't heard Cat or her mom.

Everyone around them was staring now, as interested in the drama surrounding the Calamari Kid as the game itself. The Astros pitcher had the ball back and he was preparing his next pitch. With an 0–2 count, Jalen knew it was going to be the same low inside fastball he'd thrown at Headley. It was quiet enough that he knew he could shout it out and JY would hear him, but he didn't think that was the right thing to do. If the pitcher heard him, wouldn't he change the pitch? And even if McCullers threw the inside fastball, everyone around Jalen would know what he was up to, and he doubted that was something JY wanted.

The officer didn't move an inch until McCullers threw his pitch. The big cop walked several feet toward the dugout.

Jalen saw the ball smack the catcher's mitt, but the umpire remained silent, which meant the pitch had been outside the strike zone, a ball. JY gave Jalen a desperate look. Jalen pointed toward the cop and shrugged. Cat sat back down.

Jalen shifted his attention to the pitcher, studying him and waiting for the answer to JY's question about the next pitch. It came to him late, another low inside fastball, but just as he raised his four fingers in the air, the policeman stepped in front of him again.

"Hey! Stop that!" Cat was furious.

The pitcher wound up and threw. The ball hit leather instead of wood and the ump called strike three. Without a word or a look, the officer disappeared into the dugout. JY hit the dirt with his bat and marched toward them. He looked angry and frustrated. He shook his head but said nothing.

"He just stood there." Jalen held up his hands.

JY cast an angry look into the dugout and spoke in a low voice, as if he were talking to himself. "I'm going to find out what's going on, but I'm pretty sure I already know."

"Jeffrey Foxx is what's going on," Cat growled.

49

THE GAME CONTINUED, AND THE YANKEES
struggled against McCullers.

JY didn't try and communicate with them again, so
Jalen figured they were back to the original plan, and he'd
done whatever needed to be done to ensure that the giant
police officer didn't block Jalen's view of the plate. In the
field, JY made a spectacular double play to end the top of
the fifth. The New York crowd thundered with approval,
and JY tipped his hat to them as he crossed the first base
line. He'd have his second chance at the Astros pitcher,
and there was no sign of the big policeman anywhere.

Cat had ordered some food at the top of the inning, and
it now arrived.

Her mom looked at her with surprise. "Really? You're going to eat all that?"

Cat rested a plate with two loaded hot dogs on her lap and set the large drink in her cup holder before removing its top.

"I ordered it in case I get hungry," Cat said.

Her mom frowned at the dogs oozing mustard and piled high with relish and chili. "I hope I've taught you better than to be wasteful."

"It won't go to waste." Cat jabbed her thumb in Daniel's direction. "We've got the bottomless pit in case anything's left."

Daniel leaned forward. "I hope you're not trying to disrespect my healthy appetite."

"Would I dis you about anything?" Cat asked.

Before Daniel could reply, JY emerged from the dugout with his bat, tugging on a glove. He took a few swings in the circle while McCullers threw his warm-up pitches.

The ump looked at JY. "Here we go."

JY gritted his teeth and glanced back at Jalen with a quick look that seemed to say, *Let's do this*.

Then he headed for home plate.

Jalen shifted his attention toward the pitcher's mound. McCullers studied JY with a smug grin. JY took a practice swing and paused in front of the box, looking Jalen's way.

Jalen gazed at the pitcher, eager for the identity of the next pitch. His armpits began to sweat and his face grew warm. McCullers was going to lead with his fastball.

The cop darted out of the dugout and planted himself directly in front of Jalen.

Jalen's hand shot up, but too late.

The pitcher threw his fastball. JY didn't even swing.

"Strike!"

"What?" The word escaped Jalen's lips.

To Jalen's surprise, Cat sat calmly. He leaned close so no one else could hear him. "Cat, what are we going to do?"

"Just watch the pitcher," Cat said.

"But—"

"Just *watch*," she insisted in a whisper. "Tell me when you know the pitch. When I say 'go,' we switch seats."

Jalen didn't see how that would work—the officer would simply take one step sideways to move in front of him again. But he did as he was told and focused on McCullers. The pitcher was shaking off a signal from the catcher, but Jalen couldn't see the catcher, or JY for that matter. The cop was completely blocking his view of home plate.

Jalen read another fastball coming, and excitement flooded his chest. "Okay."

"Ready? Go!" Cat shot up out of her seat and, to Jalen's total surprise, tossed the plate of food in the air.

When the dogs landed on the back of the police officer's neck, he ducked and spun around, pawing at the mess. Cat stepped in front of Jalen. Jalen slipped into Cat's seat and held four fingers up in front of his chest. JY saw Jalen's signal and stepped into the box with an eager grin. Jalen knew what JY could do with a fastball when he knew it was coming. The pitch would sail in straight and true, and that was the way it would go out if JY caught it.

"Agghh!"

The police officer's bellow as he pawed at the mess registered in the back of Jalen's mind, but his eyes were on the pitch. As predicted, it came in straight and red hot.

JY reared back and swung for the moon.

50

THE CRACK OF JY'S BAT ELECTRIFIED THE ENTIRE stadium.

With the fans on their feet and the thunder of applause washing over him, JY took off on an easy jog around the bases.

"I am *so* sorry." Cat's shouted apology to the policeman sounded sincere. "I guess I got too excited."

The officer scowled at Cat as he wiped a blob of mustardy chili from the inside of his shirt collar. Rage colored his face, but he said nothing as he skulked off into the dugout and disappeared into the stadium tunnel.

One of the hot dogs had rebounded back at Daniel, and he had evidently caught it. As the three friends high-fived,

Daniel munched on the naked dog like a carrot. He peered over the wall at the dog on the ground and held his up. "At least I saved one of them."

Cat lifted a bun from where it had landed on the top of the wall, sloppy with mustard, chili, and relish. She raised her voice above the crowd. "How about a roll?"

"Sure." Daniel took it from her, slapped the dog into it, and took a giant bite, before speaking loudly with a full mouth. "Iss chili iss killer."

Jalen's laughter blended into the applause, and he leaned toward Cat so she'd be able to hear him. "That was awesome! Like a circus act."

"Yeah, like a juggling clown. I hope the GM saw it. But it won't work twice in a row, so we'll have to think of something else for JY's next at bat."

"You think the cop will be back?" Jalen asked.

"Him or someone," Cat said. "They'll do *something*. That's how Foxx is, relentless."

JY walked past them now, giving two thumbs up and a smile to the three friends before offering Cat's mom another quick wink as he disappeared into the dugout.

"He got his money's worth on that one." Cat folded her arms and sat down in her seat.

They settled back into the game. The Yankees collected a few hits off McCullers, but JY's home run was the only score. JY got up again at the bottom of the eighth inning, and by then, Cat had all four of them—including her mom—ready to signal JY based on who could see him if the big cop tried to block Jalen. When JY marched out to home plate and there was no sign of the giant officer, Jalen looked around nervously.

"What's wrong?" Cat asked, speaking low between just the two of them.

"Just what you said about Foxx," Jalen whispered as he tried to turn his attention to the pitcher. "I can't believe he's doing nothing."

"Yeah, well, focus on McCullers." Cat pointed toward the pitcher's mound. "Don't let him get into your head."

"Okay," Jalen said. "I won't."

"Good," said Cat, slapping his leg. "You got this."

Jalen stared at the pitcher. "Umm . . ."

"Jalen?" Cat had an edge to her voice now. "The ump is calling JY into the box."

Jalen's eyes shifted to home plate, where JY looked calm and cool even though his eyes were glued to Jalen as he stepped up to the plate.

"He's gonna throw it." Cat's voice was an urgent hiss.

"I *know!*" Jalen growled through his teeth. He wanted to signal something, anything, but he knew no signal was better than the wrong one.

"Strike!" hollered the umpire.

For a moment Jalen wondered how everything had suddenly gone so wrong.

But then he knew.

51

CAT HAD BEEN RIGHT.

Foxx *had* gotten into his head.

Jalen had been so worried about the policeman and the signals and who would have to make them and whether it would work that it had scrambled his concentration. His genius suddenly felt like a flickering basement lightbulb, leaving him mostly in the dark and uncertain of what he actually saw when he did see anything.

He sat there, willing himself to know, but the harder he tried, the thicker the fog in his brain seemed to get.

"Amigo," Daniel whispered, "what is going on? You gotta help him."

"I know what I have to do, Daniel," Jalen growled as McCullers went into his windup. "But I *can't*."

"Strike!" yelled the ump.

Jalen didn't stop trying, but all he could do was sit and silently root for JY while Cat wrung her hands and Daniel gritted his teeth.

The Yankees star fought back from the 0–2 count to a 3–2 full count that kept him swinging to protect the plate and stay alive. He'd glance Jalen's way before each pitch, but Jalen could only shake his head. JY sent five balls foul off his bat before McCullers got him good with a curve that dropped from JY's eyes to his knees over the last ten feet.

"Strike!"

Jalen didn't want to see James Yager's face as he stomped back to the dugout, but he felt he had to. He met Yager's burning eyes with an apologetic look as he mouthed the word, *Sorry*.

JY bit his lower lip and shook his head.

"I tried!" Jalen blurted out without thinking. All that did was darken JY's face before he looked away.

The next two Yankees batters got on—Gregorius with a single and Ellsbury on a walk—before Astros manager A. J. Hinch walked out to the mound to yank McCullers.

After a few moments, the two men walked off the diamond as Tony Sipp jogged on.

"Maybe a new pitcher will help." Cat said, looking hopefully at Jalen.

"He's got a low-nineties four-seam fastball and a decent slider," Jalen said. "And they've got him using a splitter, too."

"So you can get a feel for him," Daniel said. "Before JY gets up again."

"If he gets up," Cat replied.

"You gotta think positive." Daniel gave her a scowl.

Joe Ros struck out, and Cat stuck her tongue out at Daniel.

"You think that's helping?" Daniel glowered. Aaron Hicks stepped up to the plate with two outs and two on when Jalen surprised even himself by saying, "Slider."

Sure enough, Sipp threw a slider.

"Yes!" Cat slapped Jalen and Daniel high fives. "You got this."

Jalen sat back and exhaled. "I do. I really do. . . . Splitter."

It was a splitter. Hicks swung and got a piece of it, a side-winding dribble to the left of the mound. Sipp jumped on it, spun, and fired the ball to third base. His throw was off by a mile, sailing past the third baseman until it rebounded off the wall. The left fielder was on a full sprint to pick up the errant throw, but Gregorius's arms and legs were a blur. He rounded third and slid into home plate in a cloud of dust just as the throw arrived.

Fifty thousand necks stretched toward the umpire.

"Safe!"

Jalen and his friends jumped for joy. It was a 2–2 game, and the Yankees were at the top of their order.

Even though Tollerson ended the inning with an out on a pop fly, the Yankees had a fresh breath of life heading into the ninth.

They took the field with Bode Gutchess on the mound. The veteran with five different pitches gave up a home run to Carlos Correa on a 3–2 count but settled in to make quick work of the next three Astros batters, and the Yankees piled into their dugout with a roar. The entire stadium felt a comeback.

Sipp sat Tyler Hutt down with a nasty splitter on an 0–2 count before Reuben Hall banged one off the left-field wall for a double. Jalen correctly called each pitch that Sipp threw.

Then Headley was up, and for some reason Sipp began to unravel. With a 2–0 count, he threw a pitch so wild Hall could have jogged to third on his steal.

With a 3–0 count, Sipp grabbed his elbow. The Astros manager walked out to the mound and replaced Sipp with Ken Giles, Houston's young closer.

"I heard he threw a pitch a hundred and two against Tampa a few weeks ago," Cat said, her eyes glued to the pitcher on the mound.

"A hundred and one," Jalen said, staring himself. "And he's got a nice slider he mixes in. He's a good one."

After a few practice pitches, Giles nodded to the umpire, and Headley stepped back into the batter's box.

"What's he gonna throw?" Daniel asked.

Jalen tried to soak up every movement the pitcher made, every look, every twitch. "I don't know."

Giles threw a ninety-eight-mile-an-hour fastball that nicked the low inside corner of the plate. Headley swung, caught just the top of the ball, and two-hopped it to the second baseman, who checked Hall at third before tossing it to first for an easy out.

With the tying run on third and two outs, it was a pressure cooker when JY stepped up. It was what every big-time baseball player loved, the opportunity to win it all with the grim specter of being the loser hovering in the back of his mind.

JY took the doughnut off his bat and tossed it outside the on-deck circle. He gave Jalen a questioning look.

Jalen's stomach twisted itself into a knot.

He felt nothing but panic.

52

JY HUFFED AND TURNED AWAY.

He marched to the plate with both hands on his bat and took a practice swing before taking another look at Jalen.

"Just relax," Cat said. "You got this."

Cat was right. Jalen knew he had to relax, but knowing and doing were two different things. The harder he tried, the fuzzier things got.

Giles threw a burner. JY swung, and it fouled off his bat up and over the netting into the stands behind the plate. The scoreboard lit up with the pitch's speed: 100.

Cat leaned close to Jalen and said, "He only really has a fastball and a slider. What do you think?"

Jalen's eyes ached from the strain. "I don't know, Cat."

JY glanced over at them, but Jalen could only shake his head. Giles threw the slider too low for a strike, and JY thankfully let it pass.

"Come on, Jalen. You can do this." Cat sounded upbeat and lighthearted, but Jalen knew she was faking.

The next pitch had more heat, high and outside. JY let it by, but the ump called it a strike. JY complained, maybe to buy Jalen more time.

"It's gotta be a fastball or a slider, right?" Cat gripped Jalen's arm.

"Yeah, that's all he's got."

"Then guess," Cat said. "It's fifty-fifty. That's better than nothing."

"No, it's not, Cat." Jalen recalled JY's instructions earlier *never* to guess. "Let me concentrate."

"You've *got* to." She shook his arm. "It'll give him the best chance. Jalen, the game is on the line here."

"Cat, stop." Jalen ached to know the pitch. Cat wasn't helping.

"Signal fastball," Cat said. "That's probably what it is. Do it, Jalen, or I will."

"You?" Jalen's mouth fell open, and he couldn't help looking at her. There were two outs. The score was 3–2 with the tying run on third. JY only needed a hit to drive it in. Another home run would win it right then.

Cat turned to JY, holding four fingers up in front of her.

JY nodded and quickly turned his attention to the pitcher.

"Cat, no," Jalen said.

It was too late.

53

GILES WOUND UP AND THREW.

JY swung for the wall.

The ball—a nasty slider—snapped into the catcher's mitt, ending the game.

JY's jaw dropped in disbelief. He blinked at the ump like a man waking from a dream. Then his face warped into rage. He marched directly toward Jalen. No one else seemed to notice or care. The game was over, and many of the fans had work the next day so they were on their feet, shuffling for the exits.

Although JY didn't shout, the tone of his voice was enough to melt glass. "Are you serious? You guessed, didn't you?"

Jalen had so much to say that he ended up saying nothing, unless a garbled choking sound counted for anything.

"Just what I told you never to do," said JY through gritted teeth. "I thought it was gonna be his slider. I was *ready* for his slider until you said *fastball*."

JY turned to Cat's mom and his face softened. "Could you take these guys home? Don't wait for me. I'm not going to be good company tonight, and besides . . ."

JY turned his attention back to Jalen, looking more sad now than angry. "I've got to figure out where I go from here. I think this lucky calamari thing is about played out."

He disappeared into the dugout.

Jalen felt the world crashing in all around him.

54

JALEN LOOKED OUT THE BACKSEAT WINDOW AT
the darkness speeding past.

Cat's mom's Range Rover hit a bump in the road.

He tried to stay quiet, but occasionally he couldn't help
a muffled sniff. Tears spilled from his eyes at random
moments when the jabs of pain were particularly sharp.
Those came mostly when he thought of his mom. She was
out there, somewhere, but now he might never know her,
never get to make her proud enough to call him her son.

Even if JY paid him for tonight, he had to think that the
Yankees player might cut the fee after getting the information on only one of his four at bats. Maybe he wouldn't
advance the Bronxville travel team fees for him and

Daniel—or he'd stop payment for the detective. Jalen had no way of getting his hands on that kind of money until he was a pro ballplayer himself. He didn't want to wait that long. He'd been so close. . . .

Daniel nudged him and whispered, "Hey, amigo, it's gonna be okay. JY will get over it. Cat will figure something out and we'll pick up right where we left off."

Jalen couldn't bring himself to answer. If he started talking, he knew what would come out. He'd blast Cat for what she'd done. Breaking JY's trust by calling the wrong signal made the whole thing beyond fixing.

Daniel held his fist in the air, waiting for Jalen to bump it. Jalen turned back to the window, but that brought him no comfort. He knew how loyal Daniel was, and when he turned back, he wasn't surprised to see his friend's fist still hanging there in the air, lit by the feeble glow from the Range Rover's instrument panel.

He gave Daniel's fist a bump, then turned back to the dark outside.

When they pulled up to the Silver Liner, Cat's mom asked, "Here, or could I take you to your house, Jalen?"

"This is good, thank you," Jalen said. "I'll go help my dad."

He thanked Cat's mom for everything, anxious to get away.

"Oh, you know I love helping you kids with all this baseball stuff," she said, turning around in her seat. "It's fun. And Daniel's right about what he said—don't you worry about James. He'll come around."

Jalen thanked her again and said good-bye without trying to address Cat, because she was huddled up in the front seat and in a mood.

As he watched them drive away, Jalen wondered if his own mom would be as kind and generous as Cat's. He knew his dad wasn't really expecting him to help this late at the diner, so, after the taillights disappeared, he headed down the gravel road.

He walked the dark, lonely path and climbed his front steps by feel, comforted by the familiar screech of the rusty hinges on the front door. Inside, he changed into shorts and a clean T-shirt to sleep in, then heated up some leftover lasagna because he realized he hadn't eaten at the stadium and he was hungry. After he cleaned up, he got into bed with his book, hoping to fall asleep. He resisted the temptation to use his phone to see what people were saying on the sports sites or on social media about JY's *un*lucky collapse and the Yankees loss.

He was grateful for a book he could get lost in, *Throwback 07*, a story about a young football player who time-traveled back to the days of Jim Thorpe to play on his team. He realized he had begun to doze when he heard his father come in through the front door.

"Jalen!"

"In here!" Jalen bolted upright and the book spilled to the floor.

His father appeared in the doorway to Jalen's bedroom, his small round glasses foggy and his face flushed with emotion. "Did you hear?"

"Hear what?" Jalen couldn't read his father's face.

"About Mr. JY," his father said. "On the Twitter. The people at the Silver Liner, they all talking about it, his tweet. . . ."

"His tweet about what?" Jalen had a sinking feeling, and he thought for a fleeting moment that he might just be having a bad dream.

"About you, Jalen," his dad said. "About you and the Silver Liner . . ."

55

"WHAT . . ." JALEN TRIED TO SWALLOW, BUT HIS
mouth was too dry. "What did he say?"

Now his father's face burst into a smile and he
beamed with pride. "He said that the *reason* he not win
the game tonight because he no eat the calamari! Jalen,
it is like the first time he tweet about the Silver Liner.
Everybody is talking about it. People were coming in so
late I finally had to say no because I'm running out of
the food."

Jalen's dad gave him a tight hug, lifting him off the bed.
"That Mr. JY, he's doing the best for my restaurant. So
much. I cannot believe it. Jalen? What's wrong?"

"It was bad for him, Dad." Jalen tried not to speak

disrespectfully to his dad. "It was a bad night for him, and an even worse night for me."

"You?" His dad looked stunned. "Because the team lose? Jalen, even the best teams they lose games, and Mr. JY hit a home run, somebody say."

"Yeah. He did hit a home run." Jalen felt a bit lighter at the thought of it: a home run and batting one for four wasn't a disaster, but when JY needed it most, Jalen had failed him.

"See?" His father lightly slapped Jalen's arm. "Is a good night for everybody. Jalen, you gotta look at what you got, not what you don't got. That's no way to live your life."

His father's face grew serious. "Look at you and me. We don't got the big mansion, but we got a roof, and she's not leaking. We don't got a fancy car, but we got the van, and she gets us where we gotta go. And you got me, and I got *you*.

"Okay, you go back to sleep." His father gave him a final hug and kissed him on both cheeks. "Tomorrow is a big day. I got the money people from Goldman Sachs coming, and we gonna sign some papers to make the franchise. Maybe you help me in the morning unloading the seafood."

"You mean go with you to the market?" Jalen picked up his book, placed it on the nightstand, and got into bed.

"No, no," said his dad. "I don't go to the market no more.

The market comes to me. Now they say to me, 'Fabio, you relax, we bring you what you need. Only the best.'"

Jalen laughed. "That's nice, Dad. That's real nice."

"Yes, that's what happens when you got a famous New York Yankee tweeting about you restaurant."

That idea didn't help Jalen get to sleep. Instead he tossed and turned beneath his covers, tortured by questions. Was he finished with JY? Where would more money for Emery Moore come from? Would JY gave him another chance? Could Cat explain what had really happened, and would JY even listen? It wasn't until the small hours of the morning that he finally dropped off to sleep and dreamed about baseball and his mom.

56

JALEN SNIFFED HIS HANDS AS HE MARCHED UP Old Post Road. He wrinkled his nose because they still smelled like clams and fish, even though he'd washed them thoroughly. He hoped his friends—especially JY— wouldn't notice.

He didn't want to be too upbeat, but he couldn't help feeling a glimmer of hope when he'd gotten Cat's text saying that they were going to meet with JY at his house later that morning. When he'd asked what was going on, she told him to just meet them, and she'd explain. Jalen joined Cat and Daniel at the gates to the mansion, and Cat led them up the driveway and around to the back, where JY was stretched out on a lounge chair, wearing sunglasses and a bathing suit. His ears were stuffed with buds whose wires connected to his phone. Birds sang from the trees surrounding the pool. JY's dogs barked from inside the house, and the sound was loud enough to send a chill up Jalen's back.

Cat grabbed JY's big toe and gave it a shake.

The Yankees star jumped and swiped the glasses off his face. "Huh? What? You?"

"Yes." Cat frowned at him. "Here we are."

"Here you are. Great." JY's face gave nothing away. He pulled a T-shirt on, then waved to some deck chairs, directing them to sit. His scruffy beard had been shaved clean and his jaw, like his eyes, was sharp. "I guess I should offer you a drink, invited or not."

"Of course you should." Cat looked around expectantly. "And since when do friends need an invitation?"

Daniel looked over at the sliding glass doors leading into JY's house. The two dogs were roaring and throwing themselves repeatedly against the glass. "They can't get out, can they?"

"What? Oh." JY cupped his hands and hollered toward the house. "Butch! Missy! Down!"

The dogs went silent, but Jalen saw their shadows circling beyond the glass doors like sharks in a tank.

JY ducked behind the cabana bar and opened the

fridge. "I've got Coke, Orange Crush, or 7UP."

"I'll take an iced tea," Cat said.

"Of course you will." JY frowned and dug into the fridge. "And . . . I've got one."

He cracked open the can and handed it across the bar. "Boys? If you're going to disrupt my privacy, you might as well do it in style."

"Orange Crush," Daniel said.

"Same," said Jalen.

JY removed three cans of orange soda and came back around the bar. He handed them their sodas before reclining back in his lounge chair with a can of his own. "So, here we are."

"We came to explain what happened." Cat took a drink from her can of tea before launching into an explanation of how she had signaled him the night before against Jalen's specific instructions.

JY took a deep breath and let it out slowly. "Well, I'm glad you didn't just ignore what I asked you. So, you want the good news first or the bad news?" he asked.

"Always get the bad news first," said Cat.

"Okay," JY said, nodding at that wisdom. "I'm out of the lineup for the next two nights."

"Why?" Jalen asked. He felt sick because he was responsible.

JY chuckled. "I don't know why I'm laughing. It's certainly not funny, but they're letting Charlie Cunningham play out the rest of the series with the Astros. I'll just sit there and watch."

"You're done?" Cat was on her feet. "That's not fair! He lied! That rotten Foxx. You were supposed to have that extension already! You batted a thousand in those three games last week, and he promised. We've got to go to the media and let people know. We'll tell them everything. You can't go down without a fight."

"I couldn't agree with you more," JY said. "About the fighting part."

"Oh. Good." Cat relaxed in her chair.

"What's the good news?" Jalen asked.

"The good news is that I think that home run you helped me get last night kept me hanging on by a thread. I didn't win the game with last-minute heroics like a week ago against the White Sox, but I still scored, and one for four isn't a total meltdown. So I'm going to have another chance."

Cat peered at JY. "So you're not done?"

"Not yet. My agent says he thinks Mr. Brenneck wants Foxx to extend my contract, but Foxx is dragging his feet, hoping I fall apart so he can convince Mr. B that it's a bad idea. The twist is that I think what Foxx has in mind is to have Joe put me in the lineup when he knows I'm going to be facing the other team's best pitcher."

"Like McCullers." Daniel scowled and bit his lip.

"To make it as hard as he can for me." JY put the sunglasses on and laid his head back. "So, for Boston, that means . . ."

"Rick Porcello," Cat said. "Oh boy."

"I don't know that." JY appeared strangely calm. "But I suspect that's who I'll get a shot against. It looks like he'll be pitching on Sunday. I should know sometime tomorrow."

Jalen said, "His sinker is filthy, and he throws it nearly forty-five percent of the time. . . ."

JY looked quizzical.

"Forty-four point seven percent, actually," Jalen added.

"I forgot—math genius," JY said with a chuckle.

Jalen could see the numbers in his head, and a couple of graphs as well. "He tightened up his four-seamer in 2016 so that it hits the top of the zone and spins like it's gonna go right over your head, only it doesn't. He throws that only twenty percent of the time . . . roughly."

"Yeah, that's the guy." JY huffed. "He's got a wicked slider, too, and his changeup is right up there. I could use some baseball genius against him, that's for sure."

Jalen felt as if someone had just released him from a

choke hold. "So you're paying me for last night?"

JY looked surprised. "Yeah, why wouldn't I?"

"Well, I didn't get the job done," Jalen said.

"You were there. And Cat already told me she was guilty for signaling the wrong pitch. I might not have used you again, but I still would have paid you. Besides, that money is already spent. Your travel team fees and the down payment for Emery."

"Who's Emery?" Daniel asked.

"The private detective looking for my mom." Jalen looked down at his hands, unsure why he was embarrassed. He looked up at the Yankees second baseman. "Thank you."

"Hopefully, I'll be the one thanking you." With the soda still in his hand, JY pointed at Jalen. "The question is, what are we going to do this weekend if you're playing at the same time I am? I need a commitment here."

"What do you mean?" Daniel asked.

"He means," Cat said, "what do we do if the Bandits are in the championship game on Sunday afternoon—which is likely—and at the same time the Yankees are finishing their series with the Red Sox? Right, JY?"

"That's correct." JY sipped his soda and frowned.

"Well, we gotta think positive, that's what." Cat stood up and waved her hands in the air. "We can do this. The tournament is at the Harvard athletic fields, which are only about ten minutes from Fenway, so even if you both end up playing at the same time, we are going to make this thing happen.

"It'll be like the ultimate double play."

57

THE QUIET LAKE BORDERED THE BACK SIDE OF the park. At the end of a well-worn dirt path was an enormous maple tree jutting out over the water's glassy surface. A thick horsehair rope hung from the largest branch above the water. Knotted at the end, it was the perfect swing from the high bank, and after some sandwiches at the Silver Liner, that was where the three friends decided to spend their afternoon before baseball practice that night.

With towels wrapped around their necks, they arrived at the peaceful lake with nothing to disturb them but the chatter of birds and a light breeze rippling the water's surface. They laid out their towels in a patch of sunshine.

Daniel grabbed the rope hanging from the tree branch at the water's edge and climbed the bank.

"Double, anyone?"

"You test it out," Cat said. "That lightning storm the other night may have weakened the branch, and if it breaks, someone could snap their neck, so you just go."

"Snap my *neck*?"

"She's just kidding." Jalen lay back and closed his eyes, studying the red-orange light through his lids.

"Well, I'm not going first." Daniel held out the rope for Cat.

"Why, what a gentleman," she said.

Jalen opened his eyes and watched her swing out over the water and launch herself into the air. She did a somersault before plunging cleanly into the water.

"Show-off," Daniel grumbled, retrieving the rope and preparing his own flop, which made a splash like a large tuna.

Jalen breathed deeply, listening to his friends bicker and splash each other. While the sun baked him, he thought about Emery Moore and imagined her at her computer, searching and searching, before he envisioned her flying in an airplane, cap pulled low over her serious face, heading to some remote place where she had located Jalen's mother.

Daniel pestered him to join them, as he and Cat repeatedly flew through the air and splashed into the water, but Jalen was too comfortable, relaxed, and happy.

His blissful state came to an abrupt end when he heard rough voices shouting profanities and an undercurrent of mean laughter coming from deep in the woods. Cat and Daniel were trying to dunk each other, so they were unaware of the intruders. The sour sounds spread to Jalen's stomach. Then, just as suddenly, everything went quiet, even the birds and the breeze. Jalen thought maybe the voices had traveled on the warm breeze all the way from the park, and he began to relax again.

He closed his eyes and his breathing slowed. He felt his skin growing warm enough for a swim. A cicada high up in the oak tree began to ratchet out its ugly song when, without warning, Jalen sensed people around him. He opened his eyes and shaded them with one hand, propping himself up on one elbow just as Chris Gamble kicked a cloud of dirt and small stones into his face.

58

"HEY, HEY! IT'S THE CALAMARI *QUITTER*!" CHRIS laughed and checked to see if his friends—Dirk, Brad, and two others—thought the new name was as funny as he did.

Jalen coughed and wiped the dirt from his face as he stood.

Peering past Jalen, Chris spotted Cat and Daniel down by the water's edge, and his face changed. "Hey, Cat. What are you doing with these two losers? You're too nice. You should kick them to the curb. They're used to it."

Chris's friends laughed some more.

Jalen had never seen Cat at a loss for words before, but she just blinked at Chris in disbelief.

Chris whipped off his shirt, exposing his pale, blubbery

torso. "C'mon, we can do a double on the rope."

He walked past Jalen like he didn't exist and grabbed Cat's arm to lead her up the bank to the rope.

When Cat slapped him, it sounded like a firecracker.

Chris reached up and touched the red mark on his cheek. He glowered at Cat. "What's wrong with you?"

"What's wrong with *you*?" Cat snarled. "You don't touch me. Remember?"

Furious, Jalen started moving down to the water. He didn't know what to do—but he had to do something.

"You—you—" Chris looked like his head might explode. "You freak! And you!" He pushed Daniel off his feet into the water. Daniel's clothes and towel were lying on the bank, and Chris grabbed them too, wadding everything into a big ball and flinging it into the lake as well.

Jalen stepped in front of Cat. "You don't—"

"Don't what, Calamari? Calamari *Quitter*?"

Chris's friends looked poised to strike. Jalen wished he were Chris's size, even close to it. Then he'd for sure knock his block off. As it was, he was ready to try.

Just then Daniel slogged up out of the water with his clothes and towel dripping in his hands. Everyone looked his way.

Taking advantage of the momentary lull, Cat said, "Let's get out of here. Leave them to it."

She urged Jalen and Daniel up the bank.

Walking away, they heard a *whoop* as Chris hit the water.

He broke the surface and shouted gleefully to his friends. "C'mon, you guys! It's awesome!"

Daniel grumbled and threw his wet things to the ground before heading back toward the water.

"Where you going?" Jalen whispered.

"Back to put some kung fu hot sauce on these guys." Daniel whirled around on Jalen as if he was the enemy. "We can't let them do this."

"Just stop it, Daniel," Cat scolded. "They're twice your size. They're idiots. And there are five of them. Let's just go."

"What about honor?" Daniel scrunched up his face but kept his voice low. "How can my amigo and me just crawl away like worms? It's okay for you. You're a girl."

"Oh boy." Jalen shook his head while Cat's face turned stormy. "Now you did it."

Cat grabbed Daniel by the arm and yanked him close so that their noses almost touched. She spoke in a low, furious voice. "It's *worse* when you're a girl. People are always assuming I'm weak, but I'm not. Am I?"

It wasn't a question.

"No," Daniel said, and only then did Cat turn him loose.

"Hey!" Chris shouted from the water. "Dirk, do you smell something?"

"Yeah," Dirk responded in his own loud voice. "Something stinks!"

"Smells like a couple of quitters! Ha-ha!" Chris and Dirk and the other boys all began splashing one another and howling with laughter.

Daniel reached for his clothes. "Okay, let's go."

No one said a word until they came out of the woods and began to cut across the park, heading back toward town. The sun was hot and the grass baked dry so that their feet scuffed up the dust. As they walked, Jalen looked over at Cat and was surprised to see a crooked smile on her face.

"What's that look about, Cat?" Jalen asked.

"I'm just thinking about how good it's going to feel," she said.

"How good what's going to feel?" Jalen asked.

"When you beat Chris in Boston this weekend," Cat said. "I can't wait."

59

PRACTICE THAT EVENING WITH THE BANDITS
was held at the Bronxville Middle School field.

Coach Allen greeted his two new players with a smile,
looking up from his clipboard and motioning for Jalen
and Daniel to join him in the dugout.

"Sit down for a minute, guys." Coach Allen pointed to
the bench.

Jalen twisted the strap to his gear bag nervously in
his hands. The coach leaned forward with his elbows on
his knees and looked sideways at the two friends. "Well,
I don't want to sound like I'm happy about this, but I'm
happy for you."

He looked pointedly at Daniel. "Our regular left fielder,

Derek Cantor, was skateboarding this afternoon at the park—which I tell our players not to do—and he broke his arm."

Daniel's face went from confusion to fighting back a smile. "So I'm playing?"

"Yes, but try not to look too happy about it when I announce it to the rest of the team, okay?"

"You got it, Coach." Daniel's face was serious as a gravestone.

"Okay, you guys get out there and get warmed up. We start in ten."

When they left the dugout, Daniel motioned for Jalen to follow him around back. When they were alone, Daniel pumped his feet and arms up and down like a madman running in place.

"Yessss! Yessss! Yesss!" Daniel hissed before he grabbed Jalen around the waist, lifted him off his feet, and spun him around. "I'm a Bandit. I'm a *Bandito*."

The two of them laughed together and slapped each other a couple of dozen high fives before Daniel blew out a sharp-sounding breath and they jogged out onto the field like nothing had happened.

When their new coach blew his whistle, the team surrounded him outside the dugout, and everyone took a knee. Coach Allen told his team about Derek Cantor. Then he introduced Jalen and Daniel as their new teammates, saying they were just in time for Boston the next day. He reviewed the practice plan for the evening before giving his whistle a short blast. It was all very businesslike, almost cold, and Jalen worried about fitting in.

He fell in with the rest of the players, running the bases until they were loose and warm. On the last lap, Jalen failed to slow his pace, and when he got distracted by the new surroundings, he scuffed the heel of the player in front of him. It was Grady Gertz, and with his shoe half off, Grady tumbled down the baseline in a cloud of dust. Jalen pulled up and felt the horror of messing up their team's star pitcher before practice had even begun.

Everything stopped, and no one said a word.

Jalen instinctively offered Gertz a helpful hand.

Stunned, Gertz looked up at Jalen, his eyes on fire. Jalen's hand hung in the air between them like a piece of dirty laundry.

From right behind him, Jalen heard Daniel mutter, "Oh, hot sauce."

60

GERTZ'S EYES WENT BACK AND FORTH FROM
Jalen's hand to his face before he took the hand and let
Jalen pull him to his feet. Gertz examined his legs as he
dusted off, then looked up at Jalen with a smile. "Don't
worry, I'm fine. Just make sure you run the bases this fast
in Boston. We'll score two extra runs a game if you do."

Jalen wanted to hug the other kid, but instead he nodded like a happy fool and said, "You got it."

Practice wasn't much different from the ones they had
with the Rockets, except that Coach Allen and his assistant, Coach Miller, a heavyset man with a pale bald head,
didn't yell as much. When they did raise their voices, it
was to praise someone, and that felt good to Jalen when

he ripped eight line drives in a row during live batting practice against Gertz.

"Awesome!" Coach Allen hollered.

When his turn was up, the coach took Jalen aside. "Were you doing that genius thing with Gertz?"

Jalen smiled. "His changeup is brutal unless you know it's coming."

"And you knew?" The coach raised his eyebrows. "That's pretty amazing. Okay, get out there in the field."

After practice, Gertz tapped Jalen on the shoulder. "We're all going to Häagen-Dazs. You guys should come."

"Thanks." Jalen looked at Daniel. "Will your father let us?"

"My dad?" Daniel beamed with pride. "If he's within a hundred miles of some dulce de leche, he's there."

"Great," said Gertz. "It's right on the corner of Park Place and Pondfield. We'll see you guys there."

Daniel's father took them to the ice cream shop, parking on the street a couple of blocks away. Despite the fading daylight, the town was teeming with people, young and old, and there was a long line for ice cream that went halfway down the block. Gertz was well ahead of them in line with a handful of other Bandits players, but he came back to where they stood and said, "Why don't I order for you guys. Mr. Bellone, I already know you want dulce de leche."

Gertz took all their orders and accepted a twenty-dollar

bill Daniel's dad insisted he take before they left the line to wait outside the store's exit. Gertz brought their ice cream out to them before returning with his own. Four other players trailed behind him. Everyone seemed to take their lead from Gertz, and they all fell into an easy conversation about whether the Yankees or Red Sox had the greatest franchise in baseball history.

The team's catcher, Justin Fanwell, who they all called "Fanny," led the minority who were as devoted to the Sox as the others were to the Yankees. Fanny was built like a brick, stout and solid, and his cheeks went red at the mention of the curse of the Bambino.

"Ted Williams was ten times the player Babe Ruth was," said Fanny, setting off a chorus of jeers from the Yankees fans. "Last I checked, .344 is better than .342."

"Yeah, but seven hundred fourteen is *way* better than five hundred twenty-one!" someone shouted.

"Home runs do mean more than batting average." Gertz held his raspberry sherbet ice cream cone up like a king's scepter. "Championships are what it's all about, and the Babe won seven."

"Three with Boston!" Fanny pumped a fist in the air.

"Yankees have twenty-seven titles!" Daniel was so excited, he smudged his nose with cookies and cream. "Boston has eight!"

"Let's talk twenty-first century," argued Fanny. "Boston leads 3–2 in modern times."

And so it went.

The sky beyond the glow of the streetlights had faded to black by the time they'd finished their ice cream, said good-bye, and returned to Daniel's father's truck for the ride home.

"That's a nice group of boys," Daniel's father said as he steered his truck onto the parkway. "Do you like them as much as the guys on the Rockton team?"

Daniel turned around from the front seat to make a crazy face at Jalen before they both burst out laughing.

"You two," Daniel's father said, shaking his head, "*todos locos.*"

The Silver Liner was hopping when they drove past. Even though it was nearly ten o'clock, new customers were arriving in their cars and SUVs.

"You're gonna be rich," Daniel said. "There's gonna be a Silver Liner in every city soon, amigo."

Jalen didn't comment, but he felt a bubble of joy in his throat. After thanking Daniel's father for the ride and giving his buddy a final fist bump, he let himself into his home. He had just turned on the light in his bedroom when his phone began to buzz.

It was JY, and after hello he said, "I got some good

news and some bad news. I'm going to give you the good news first."

Before Jalen could remind him that it was always best to hear the bad news first, JY continued.

"I just got off the phone with Emery. She found your mom's parents . . . your grandparents."

61

JALEN GRABBED THE FRAMED PICTURE OF HIS
mother from its shelf. Holding it in one hand and his
phone in the other, he paced the floor and held his breath,
because as good as that news was, he knew some bad
news was coming. He waited, and finally JY exhaled and
said, "The bad news is—and I'm sorry—they passed three
years ago in a car accident."

Jalen's heart froze. He studied the picture of her face, the
big dark eyes, the pretty straight nose, and tried to ignore
the crashing sound in his head. "What about . . . my mom?"

"So, good news and bad news there, too."

Jalen swallowed the panic bubbling up in his throat.
"Bad news first. Please."

"Emery hasn't found her yet, that's the bad news. Good news is that she wasn't with them in the crash. Also, the obituary in the newspaper—it's a paper down in Charleston, South Carolina—said they were survived by their only daughter, Elizabeth, who lived in London, England."

"So Emery's close to finding her?" Jalen asked.

"She told me pretty specifically to say to you that you shouldn't get your hopes up. It's always harder, I guess, to find someone when they've left the country. And it's been three years, so a lot could have happened."

Jalen felt a weight in his stomach. "Like a car crash."

"Yeah, but probably not."

"How are *you* doing?" Jalen asked, remembering his manners.

"Me? Not bad, except that I should be the one stepping up to the plate right now instead of Charlie Cunningham. Look at that kid. He doesn't even have to shave."

"You're watching the game?"

"I stepped into the clubhouse," JY said. "And . . . Oh, crap."

"What happened?"

"He just hit a double. I better go. I've been putting some bad mojo out there, and he didn't have a hit until I came in here. Darn it."

"I'm sorry."

"Not your fault, but I want to get my mojo going again. Maybe he'll get thrown out on a steal?" JY cleared his throat. "Hey, don't hate me for rooting against my own teammate, okay? I'm not proud of it, but when you're in the pros, you can't help it when someone on their way up is trying to take your job."

"I get it," said Jalen.

"Well, you will one day anyway. Talk to you later."

JY hung up, and Jalen replayed the second baseman's final words in his mind before he spoke out loud to the picture in his hands.

"One day, Mom. He said, 'one day.'"

62

JALEN PUT THE PICTURE DOWN, FEELING SILLY.

Who talked to a picture? A crazy kid, that was who.

He got into bed and opened his book. He read nearly thirty pages before he felt tired enough to turn off the light, and even then, he didn't fall asleep for a long time.

The next day, Friday, he helped his dad out at the diner in the early morning before getting a ride from Daniel's dad to Bronxville.

"I really liked practice yesterday," Daniel said as they rode along in his father's truck.

"You gotta practice to get better," Jalen said.

"Yeah, but I mean I *like* it with the Bandits, everyone being so nice."

"It's a big difference, right?" Jalen said.

When they arrived at Bronxville Middle School, where the bus was to pick them up, Jalen wondered how it would be, going to Boston. Was last night's friendly atmosphere a fluke?

While they were waiting for the bus, Jalen asked Gertz about the Häagen-Dazs. "You guys do that every night?"

"No one ever died from eating too much ice cream," Gertz said.

A couple of guys around him laughed at that and repeated it.

"Yeah," said Daniel, joining in, "not like doughnuts."

"Doughnuts?" Fanny wrinkled his brow.

"This guy in Denver tried to eat a half-pound doughnut in eighty seconds." Daniel made a throat-cutting gesture and chuckled. "Gonzo. Choked to *death*. Can't happen with ice cream, though. Ice cream melts."

"And you think that's funny?" Fanny asked. "That's pretty weird, if you do."

Everyone stopped laughing and looked at Fanny's scrunched-up freckled face.

"Easy, Fanny," said Gertz. "We're all just kidding."

And just like that, Jalen felt like he was back with the Rockets.

"Yeah?" Fanny ignored Gertz and pointed his thumb at Jalen as he stared down Daniel. "You know what I think about you and your buddy here?"

Daniel shifted his stance and raised his chin. "No. What?"

63

FANNY HELD UP A HIGH FIVE AND GRINNED. "I'D
say you fit right in with the rest of us weirdos."

Everyone laughed, and they began to call out Fanny's
name in a way Jalen knew was an old routine.

"That's my Fanny!" someone called.

"No, that's *my* Fanny!"

"Keep your hands off my Fanny!"

"That's one freckled Fanny!"

"Everyone loves a red-haired Fanny!"

Laughter finally drowned out the shouts, and the bus
arrived.

On their way across the parking lot to the bus, Jalen
whispered, "I was worried for a minute there with that

choking thing. It was like we were back with the Rockets."

"The Rockets are rotten," Daniel said. "I knew he was kidding. This is what a team is supposed to be, laughing and joking."

"You *knew*?" Jalen shook his head. "You mean that wasn't the beginning of a flying-crane stance you were in?"

"What would you know about a flying crane?"

"Only what you tell me." Jalen tossed his gear into the belly of the bus.

"Kung fu can't be contained," Daniel said. "I wasn't concerned, but my kung fu sometimes takes over so that I'm always prepared."

"Oh, I get it." Jalen bit back a smile, and they piled onto the bus.

The long ride was filled with laughs and joking. At some point, Daniel moved to sit with Fanny, and Jalen wound up with Gertz.

They were getting along great. Still, Jalen was surprised when Gertz nudged him and said, "Hey, Jalen. How about you and me room together in Boston? I know you and Daniel are best friends, but he can room with Fanny, and that way you guys can learn the ropes."

"Yeah, that sounds great. Let me just make sure with Daniel, okay?"

Daniel was busy watching Fanny show him how to fold

a handbill into a streamlined paper airplane, and Jalen couldn't catch his attention.

"If he's not cool with it, that's okay too," Gertz said. "I was just thinking it'd help you guys feel like part of the team more, since the rest of us have been playing together for a couple years already."

When Jalen was sitting with Daniel again, he got to ask the question.

Daniel laughed. "That's funny. I was going to ask you the same thing. I didn't want to hurt your feelings, but Fanny said he could help me get the lay of the land so I didn't feel like a rookie. Jalen? Who *are* these guys?"

Jalen sighed. "I don't know, but I'm glad we found them."

"Well, technically they found you."

"You think most teams are like this?" Jalen asked. "Ice cream and laughing and friendly, or like the Rockets?"

Daniel said, "I think this is exactly what a team is supposed to be like."

They rode for a few moments just looking at each other, until Jalen asked, "You thinking what I'm thinking?"

"How good it'll be if we play the Rockets at this tournament?" Daniel said.

"Not just play them," Jalen said. "How about if we beat their pants off?"

64

THE BUS FINALLY REACHED BOSTON, AND THE
Bandits got off at the Charles Hotel in Cambridge, right
near Harvard Square. There was a Shake Shack around
the corner, and the ball fields were a short walk across
the Anderson Memorial Bridge. Cat and her mom were
going to be staying at the same hotel so Cat could keep the
books for the team during their games.

During the ride, Cat had been texting back and forth
with Jalen to keep him up to speed on JY and what the
three-day Boston trip was looking like for him. Jalen was
hoping JY would get into the lineup that night, because
his own team didn't have a game until Saturday morning.
If he could help JY during the Yankees game Friday night,

he might have the rest of the weekend to focus on his own team, but that wasn't to be. Cat texted to tell him that JY wouldn't be in the lineup until Sunday's game at one p.m.

"Look." Jalen showed Daniel his phone. "They're playing JY against Porcello on Sunday."

"Well, he figured that," Daniel said as they grabbed their bags from under the bus. "So, why do you look like the world ends in sixty seconds?"

Jalen pulled up a document on his phone that showed the 13U Boston tournament schedule. He held it up for Daniel to see. "Look when the championship game is."

"Oh, wow," Daniel said. "Three o'clock. You won't be done with the Yankees by then. And . . . the Rockets are in the other bracket? So if we play them at all, it'll be in the championship."

Jalen bit his lip and filed inside with the rest of the team to get his room key.

"What are you gonna do?" Daniel asked. "Tell JY you can only help for the first half of the game?"

"I don't think he's gonna buy that." Jalen shook his head. "Cat said the box seats at Fenway are costing him ten grand, and then throw in my five-grand fee on top of that. I can't imagine him paying fifteen thousand dollars for me to help him out and leave after the sixth inning, or whenever it'd be."

"Well," Daniel said, "maybe we won't make it to the championship game."

"Hey, Daniel, what did you just say?" Gertz burst in between them with his room key in hand. "Maybe we won't *make it* to the championship? I don't know about your old team, but this is the Bronxville Bandits. We *always* make it to the championship game."

Gertz wasn't being unpleasant, just reciting a historical fact.

"Of course." Daniel's face reddened, and he forced a laugh. "Bandits. Championships. I forgot which team I'm on now."

"That's the spirit." Gertz turned to Jalen. "Come on, roomie, let's catch the first elevator."

The coaches had given them only fifteen minutes to settle in before they were to meet in the lobby. Jalen and Daniel followed Gertz through the lobby to the elevator bank and stepped onto the first one that opened. Fanny hustled aboard too. The doors were closing when a hand reached in to stop them.

"No room!" Fanny yelled.

When the doors parted on Coach Allen's grim face, Fanny said, "Sorry, Coach. Didn't know it was you."

"I think your good manners should extend to everyone, Fanny. Not just your coaches. You represent this team."

The coach let his stern gaze linger on Fanny before he turned his eyes to Jalen. "Jalen, put your stuff in your room and then head right down to the lobby. You and I need to talk."

The doors began to close again, but this time Coach Allen let them go.

The elevator doors thumped shut and as the car began to move, Fanny said, "Uh-oh."

65

"WHAT WAS THAT ALL ABOUT?" WHISPERED
Fanny as the elevator rose. "It didn't look good."

"Oh, he always gets uptight before a tournament." Gertz
tried to wave the tension away with his hand as he turned
to Jalen. "You'll be fine."

The bell dinged and they all got off on seven.

"I don't know," said Fanny as he led the way down the
hall. "Coach doesn't normally scold the Fanny."

"Dude, you screamed 'no room' when there were four
of us on the elevator." Gertz stuck the key in his door.

"The Fanny likes a little privacy." Fanny turned toward
his own door across the hall. "Coach has to understand
that."

Jalen dumped his gear bag and his duffel on the bed by the window and turned to go.

"Want me to go with you?" Gertz asked.

"I better go alone," Jalen said. "But thanks, Gertzy."

Downstairs, Coach Allen sat on one of the lobby couches, busy on his phone.

"You wanted to see me, Coach?"

"Hey. Yeah, grab a seat." Coach Allen spoke in a pleasant tone and that allowed Jalen to relax a bit. "So, I heard from JY that he'd to like you to be at the Red Sox game on Sunday."

"I know," Jalen said. "And the championship game is supposed to start at three o'clock."

"If you're helping JY Sunday, and we make it to the championship, you'll miss at least half our game, maybe most or all of it," said the coach. "Jalen, look, I know JY paid your fee, and it's important that you help him out, but when he and I spoke, he said I might have to make some accommodations for practice. This is a pretty big game. Now, I'm not going to tell you what to do here, but I do think you're going to have to make a decision soon on whether you want to be a baseball *player* or a baseball genius. You've got a nice bat, and your ability to focus in the field along with some quick feet gives you a huge upside on defense, but all these things need to be developed, and you can't do that while you're in the stands watching the Yankees. Do you get what I'm saying?"

"Yes, Coach."

"It's too bad it didn't work out for tonight," Coach Allen said. "That would've been perfect, right?"

"Yes."

"Well, you'll get to see the Yankees anyway."

"Coach?"

"I'm surprising the team." Coach Allen stood. "We're going to Fenway for tonight's game. You ever seen the Green Monster?"

"On TV."

"Well, you're in for a treat," the coach said. "Oldest active ballpark in America. I love this place."

Cat arrived in time to join the team for burgers at Shake Shack before they got back on the bus and crossed the river to Fenway Park. The streets around the stadium were narrow and buzzing with people. Restaurants and storefronts all had a baseball association. The pale green ribs of the Green Monster's steel skeleton rose up and jutted out over the street like some mad carnival ride. Red-and-blue caps and clothes dominated the landscape, but there was an occasional navy Yankees cap or a white pinstriped jersey in the sea of Red Sox fans.

The bus let them out into the swarm of fans and the

swirl of smells dominated by sausages, beer, and cotton candy. The team followed their coaches in through a brick archway, past the ticket takers, and up the stairs into the green-seated grandstands behind right field. When they got to their section, Coach Allen handed each of them a ticket stub.

Cat stopped in front of Jalen. "Wait, row thirty-seven?"

She peered down the row and turned back to Jalen. "Have you got seat twenty-one?"

Jalen looked at the stub Coach Allen had randomly given him. "Yeah."

"No way." Cat took the ticket and looked at it. "You do. The red seat. Do you know how lucky that is? That is so lucky."

"Why? What's the red seat?" Daniel asked from behind Jalen.

"It's the Ted Williams seat," she said. "On June 9, 1946, Ted Williams hit the longest home run ever in Fenway Park. Five hundred and two feet, and they put a red seat where it hit. Can you believe that? Over seventy years ago and no one has ever hit it that far again."

"It's good luck, amigo," Daniel said as they edged down the row to their seats.

"It's *great* luck," Cat said.

They sat down with everyone and watched the game.

But whatever luck Jalen got from the red seat didn't extend to the Yankees. The Red Sox smoked them 7–0, and as expected, JY didn't get any action. The team filed out and walked several blocks to meet their bus. On the way back to the hotel, Jalen called his dad. Even though it was late, his father was still in the thick of things at the diner, so Jalen said good night, and his father wished him luck. Jalen held off telling him about the lucky red seat, still hoping some of the luck might rub off. It was eleven o'clock by the time they got back, and everyone turned in right away.

Jalen was lying in the dark with his eyes open when Gertz asked him if he was awake.

"I can't stop thinking about tomorrow."

"Well, that's normal." Gertz's voice rang out clearly in the dark. "It's a big day for you. It's the beginning of a new chapter. It's the beginning."

"The beginning?" Jalen asked. "Of what?"

"Of your new life."

Jalen wanted to ask Gertz why he said that with so much confidence. Why did his new friend believe that this time, in this place, everything would turn out right?

He'd love to have that feeling.

Jalen wouldn't say that out loud, though. Instead he slept, troubled by dreams of strikeouts, bad restaurant reviews, and the funeral of the grandparents he'd never known.

66

THE BANDITS' FIRST GAME THE NEXT DAY WAS
against a team from Havertown, Pennsylvania. They were
a tall team, every one of them, with a tall coach, and that
made the Bandits look like a ragtag bunch, until they
began to play. When the score was 14–2, Coach Allen put
Daniel in the game to pitch.

"Let's see what you got," said the coach.

Daniel sprinted to the mound and threw his first pitch
so wild that Fanny couldn't even get his glove on it. The
Bandits all laughed in a good-natured way, and Coach
Allen cupped his hands and raised his voice. "You'll be
fine, Daniel. One pitch at a time. Just relax."

Daniel shook out his arms, took a big breath, and

blew it out. His next pitch went right down the middle, but the Havertown player caught hold of it. From second base Jalen leaped into the air, stretched his glove, and snagged it. The bleachers erupted with applause, and his teammates and coaches showered him with praise.

Daniel turned and grinned at him from the mound. "I'll set them up, and you knock them down."

"You got it, amigo," Jalen replied, giving him a thumbs-up.

Daniel gave up four hits and one run in that final inning, but he got out of a tight spot at the end to seal the win, and his new teammates swamped him with back slaps and high fives. For his part, Jalen had hit a home run and a single, striking out just once and walking once. He also made several nice plays in the field.

They had pizza for lunch at a place just off Harvard Square, then spent some time by the pool before their second game later in the day. Cat's mom appeared and showed her and Jalen the three tickets JY had secured for them for Sunday.

"They're in the same spot as the ones he got for us at Yankee Stadium, right up against the wall near the dugout." Cat's mom frowned. "He wouldn't even tell me how much they cost. It must have been a lot. He also asked me to remind you to hold the four-fingers sign under your chin if you think it's going to come in high. Does that make sense to you?"

"Yup," Jalen said. "I got it."

The Bandits won their late afternoon game, but only by a 5–3 score, and Coach Allen put Gertz in to finish the last inning and seal the win. They had been keeping Gertz in reserve, saving him to start in the championship game if they got there.

The tournament organizers were based in Dillon Fieldhouse, next to the ball fields. Outside was a big board with all the brackets for the various age groups. On it were the results, and after their second game, Jalen saw that the Bandits and the Rockets were on a collision course for the finals. The Bandits had to beat a team from Buffalo, New York, and the Rockets one from Portland, Maine, to make it happen.

Everyone talked about the tournament and what it would be like to play Rockton for the second time in a row while Daniel kept them all entertained with his scouting report on their former team.

"Watch out for their ace pitcher, Chris Gamble." Daniel's voice sounded like he was telling a ghost story. "He's the coach's son, and his breath could knock down a dinosaur."

Everyone laughed. They crossed the bridge beneath

the darkening sky, with downtown Boston glimmering at them from the distance, and the river below. A comfortable breeze slipped past, and without thinking, Jalen put his arm around Cat's shoulders and gave her a squeeze.

Almost instantly he felt silly, but when she leaned her head against his shoulder, he knew it was all right. Still, when Daniel turned around to ask Jalen if he should tell the story about how they put rabbit poo in Chris's lunch bag, Jalen dropped his arm quickly and told him to go ahead and tell it, and the Bandits players howled with delight.

"So, I'm not just a fabulous pitcher." Daniel chuckled. "I'm an expert joker, too."

"You're no Fanny, though," someone said, kicking it off.

"Who's talking about my Fanny?"

"Let's save the Fanny talk for later. There's a lady present."

"Ladies like a good Fanny."

"Just don't touch my Fanny."

They laughed and talked, and in the twilight, it felt magical to Jalen, like a band of friends lost in time and space. Everyone voted for another meal at Shake Shack before walking back to the hotel. They entered the hotel lobby in one big group, bubbling with laughter and making all kinds of noise until Coach Allen gave his whistle a short toot to get their attention and told them all to get right up to their rooms.

"Bed check in thirty minutes," he barked. "We've got a big day tomorrow."

When Cat got off the elevator on the fourth floor, where she and her mom were staying, she turned and said good night to everyone, but Jalen was pretty certain when their eyes met that she was saying something more to him without actually saying it. Like, they were best friends forever.

After watching the Yankees drop their second game to the Red Sox by a 3–1 score, Jalen said good night to Gertzy and put out the light. When his phone buzzed, he read the text to him and Cat. It was from JY, asking if they were ready for tomorrow. Jalen didn't know if he was ready, but he was so tired from a long day of baseball that he felt himself drifting off immediately. And it wasn't JY or Daniel or Chris that his last thoughts were about. They weren't even about his mom.

Instead he thought about Cat.

67

THEIR GAME AGAINST BUFFALO WAS THE FIRST
time slot Sunday morning, but it went as planned. The
Bandits got on top early and stayed there. They celebrated
with a chant after shaking hands, but the festive air from
the night before was gone. The Rockets were playing Portland on the main field at eleven o'clock, and the Bandits
marched right over there to watch so they'd be prepared
to face the winner in the championship at three o'clock.

It felt weird to Jalen to be rooting *for* Dirk and Chris
and Caleb, but he needed the Rockets to defeat Portland.
It was the only way the Bandits could smash them in the
finals. Gertzy's arm was well rested—they hadn't needed
him to throw a single pitch against Buffalo—and Jalen

knew that even with Chris at his very best, the Bandits could whip them.

It was a 2–2 tie late in the third inning of the Rockets game when Cat tapped Jalen's arm. "Come on. My mom's in the parking lot. It's time."

It wasn't that Jalen had forgotten he was supposed to go to Fenway Park to help JY against Porcello—he hadn't. It was just that the job of being JY's baseball genius was messing with the anticipated thrill of beating his old team and putting Chris in his place once and for all.

So when Jalen spoke, it was without thinking. "I've got to be here for the game. I've got to be."

"Wait. *What?*"

68

"COACH ALLEN TOLD ME I HAVE TO DECIDE IF I
want to be a baseball *player* or a baseball genius, Cat."
Jalen lowered his voice to keep the conversation between
the two of them.

"You can't back out!" Cat erupted, and Jalen knew by
the look on her face that he and Cat were going to have a
big problem. "What about the double play? Doing both?
We can help JY, and you can still make it back for the last
couple innings. You can do *both*."

Jalen felt pulled in two directions. "You know what they
say, when you try to do two things at once, you don't do
either of them well."

"Who even said that?" Cat's face turned red.

"I don't know. Someone did, though."

Cat was boiling over. "You made a deal. *I* made a deal, *the* deal. If JY hadn't paid the fee, you wouldn't even be here."

"I could pay him back." Jalen tried to sound casual and confident. "My dad is doing well now."

"Because *JY* made the Silver Liner famous!" Cat stuck her face right in his so her breath tickled his nose.

"I can't just walk away from my team, Cat." Jalen leaned back. "They'll need me. I can beat Chris at the plate. If I get a hit off him, it'll mess with his head. He could fall apart, and we could crush them. Do you know how sweet that would be after everything?"

Cat stared at him for a moment. "Jalen, listen to yourself. You *can't* do this. The Bandits can win this without you, but for JY . . . this could be the straw that breaks the camel's back. It could end his career."

The crack of a bat drew their attention back to the field just in time to see Chris scoop up a worm-burner, stomp on the bag at first where he was playing, pivot, and rifle the ball to second for a double play. Chris double-pumped his fists into the air and roared a battle cry worthy of his Neanderthal forefathers. Jalen *ached* to ruin his day.

But his mind was filled with thoughts of his father and the things JY had done—for them both.

His father's voice seemed to echo in his ear. *A man who don't keep his word, he's no man.*

69

JALEN TURNED TO DANIEL, WHO'D BEEN WATCH-
ing their discussion with wide eyes. He bumped fists with
his friend before heading down the aisle.

Coach Allen was sitting in the end seat a few rows
down, and as he passed him, Jalen said, "I gotta go do
that thing at Fenway, Coach. I'll be back as soon as I can.
I'm so sorry."

Coach Allen let out a heavy sigh, then frowned at Jalen.
"You do what you have to do, Jalen. Just get back as fast
as you can."

"Okay, Coach. I'll hurry. I wouldn't do it, but I promised."

Jalen and Cat walked out toward the road and stood in
the shadow of Harvard Stadium until Cat's mom pulled up

in her Range Rover. "You kids ready?" Cat's mom asked. "Exciting, right? Is something wrong?"

"Jalen's got his game face on, that's all," Cat said.

"I'm worried about getting back as fast as I can, Mrs. Hewlett. I want to help my new team beat my old team."

"I get that," Cat's mom said. "When it gets close to the end, I'll get the Rover and pull right up in front of the stadium. That way we'll beat the traffic and get right back here."

"Thank you." Jalen felt a little better, but not much. Coach Allen's words about him having to make a choice between being a player or a "genius" still rang in his ears.

Cat's mom showed them the gate where they'd meet after the game. Then she pulled into a garage right across the street. As they entered Fenway, Cat's mom stopped and pointed again at the white baseball-shaped sign on the corner that said BOSTON RED SOX. "So you'll come out of this gate, twenty. When it gets close to the end, I'll come get the Rover and pull it right out so as soon as you get here we can take off. That should get us out of any traffic."

"Thank you." Jalen appreciated that Cat's mom was taking his playing in the championship game so seriously.

Inside, they were directed to the box seat area, all the way down to the wall separating the stands from the field.

The Yankees were on the field for warm-ups, and JY saw them almost immediately, giving them a thumbs-up to go with his grin.

"Looks like he's not too worried about me reading the pitches," Jalen said, sitting down next to Cat.

"Why would he? Foxx can't have the police or anyone block your view here. You'll be fine without the distractions, right?"

"I should be."

"Positive thinking, right? You can do this." Cat sat back and chewed her gum with intensity. Usually so cool, she seemed nervous enough for both of them.

Jalen couldn't help wishing he were with his own team. It distracted him to know that in a short time they would be taking the field against Chris without him to help. It might have been that distraction that left him feeling so relaxed as the Yankees-Red Sox game began. Even though Porcello shut the top of the Yankees' order down with just ten pitches, by the time the top of the inning was over, Jalen had a bead on the Red Sox star pitcher. He signaled to JY that all was well, and it was—until JY committed an error on a routine ground ball, which led to the Red Sox taking a 1–0 lead going into the second inning.

As Gardner struggled against Porcello, JY moved to the on-deck circle.

"That error makes his batting even more important." Cat said, wringing her hands.

Jalen had the flash thought that if JY struck out, the game would end faster and let him get back to his business of being a player, but he pushed the thought away and concentrated on the pitching.

"No worries," he replied just as Gardner struck out.

"You know?" Cat looked as excited as he'd ever seen her.

"Yup." He gave JY the *okay* sign.

As JY tightened his batting glove in the circle, Jalen turned his attention back to the mound. Porcello studied JY as he stepped into the box. He shook off the catcher's signal, then nodded.

Jalen gave JY a thumbs-down gesture for the two-seam sinker. JY adjusted his feet and swung early. The bat cracked, and the grounder went wide of the third base line.

Cat groaned.

"It's okay," Jalen said, studying Porcello. "It's just one strike."

The next pitch was a four-seam and it would be high, so Jalen held the four fingers under his chin.

It was high, too high for JY to get a good piece of it, and it flew off the bat foul into the netting above Jalen.

"Jalen." Cat grabbed his arm and squeezed.

"I can't hit it for him," Jalen said. "I can only tell him what's coming."

"I know, but . . ." Cat's voice trailed off.

Jalen hesitated, uncertain what Porcello would do with his 0–2 count.

"Jalen?" Cat said. "Hurry."

70

JALEN SAW ANOTHER SINKER COMING AT THE
last instant.

He signaled, thumbs-down, but JY barely got his eyes
back to the pitcher as the ball was released. It was as nasty
as a pitch could be, dropping a foot at the last moment.

The Yankees star swung but missed, and the Boston
crowd went wild.

71

PORCELLO WAS ON FIRE.

He knocked down Yankees batters like ducks in a shooting gallery.

JY's next at bat came in the fifth inning. The Boston fans surrounding Jalen and Cat began to talk in low voices about a no-hitter.

Jalen signaled the pitches to JY, two sinkers to start. JY let them both pass. One was a strike, the other a ball.

Jalen gritted his teeth and leaned toward Cat. "He's got to *swing*."

He signaled a third straight sinker, and JY let that go as well. It was a ball, though, and the 2–1 count felt like a breath of fresh air.

"Maybe he's smarter than you think," Cat said. "Now's he up on the count."

Jalen signaled a high fastball.

JY smashed it, a frozen rope right at Porcello. In a blink, the pitcher snapped his glove around and snagged the line drive. JY banged the end of his bat in the dirt as he marched back to the dugout. Cat gave Jalen a worried look.

Jalen shrugged. "Porcello is killing it."

"You don't sound too upset."

It was just after two thirty, and Jalen wasn't going to point out that at this rate, he might be back with the Bandits in the first or second inning of the championship. He knew he was doing his best. "All I can do is signal the pitches. The rest is up to him, Cat."

"Well, he's 0 for 2," she snapped, like it was his fault. "We really need these next two at-bats to be hits."

"Or next one." Jalen nodded toward the mound. "If Porcello keeps this up, JY'll only get one more chance."

"Do you even *want* to save his career?" Cat's eyes flashed.

Jalen watched JY jog out onto the field to take up his position at second base. "Yes. I do want to help him, Cat. And I am *here*, helping him. But I want to be out there one day, and I won't be able to get there unless I put in the hard work and get the game experience. You've got to play baseball to get better. Practice isn't enough."

"Well, hopefully you can do both," she said.

"Yeah, I know," he said. "The double play. But a lot of things have to happen just right for even the *chance* to make a double play."

Over the next two innings Porcello did his part, and so did Michael Pineda, who was pitching a whopper of a game for the Yankees. He had given up only one run on three hits, but he had also sprinkled in five walks.

Pineda was leaking oil after his hundredth pitch but navigated through a scoreless seventh. Clusters of Yankees fans scattered around Fenway gave him a standing ovation.

It was the eighth inning when Porcello showed real signs of weakness. On a 3–2 count, Gregorius let a fastball go by. It was just high, and when the ump signaled ball, Fenway really got loud. The booing raged up into the warm summer afternoon as Gregorius took first. And the Yankees dugout came to life. JY had a chance to save the team from being swept in their Boston series.

"I think you're right," Cat said. "JY probably won't bat again after this. Jalen, this might really be it. If Foxx has Mr. Brenneck convinced that last week was a total fluke, JY can't get shut out. He's *got* to get a hit here. He's just got to."

Jalen gave her a nod and shifted his focus to the Red Sox pitcher. "I'll do everything I can."

72

THE WALK WOULDN'T PREVENT PORCELLO FROM
notching a shutout. Only a hit could do that. Still, the Red
Sox pitcher looked like he had a mouthful of broken glass,
and Jalen knew he was going to try and muscle his way
past JY, who'd struggled to connect with his fastball.

Jalen needed to be sure, though. He saw no reason to
rush. He knew JY was watching him carefully, so after
concentrating on the pitcher for a few more seconds, he
held four fingers under his chin. JY saw it and shifted his
feet just as Porcello went into his windup.

The fastball came in high, just as Jalen had predicted it
would. JY swung for the wall. He got around late on it, and
the ball sailed in the direction of the Pesky Pole in right

field. Cat, her mom, and Jalen jumped to their feet. Every eye in the stadium followed it. Every neck stretched.

But the ball went foul.

"Oh, he almost had it!" Cat moaned, and clapped her hands together once.

The next three pitches were high, tantalizing fastballs as well, and even though he knew they were coming, JY couldn't do more than nick them foul. His timing seemed to be off, and Porcello smelled blood like a shark in the water. With an 0–2 count, JY was fighting furiously to protect the plate, and it seemed like he was getting less and less of the ball.

"That last one was ninety-seven miles per hour," Cat's mom said.

Cat followed the direction of her mother's finger, pointing to the pitch speed on the scoreboard, before she turned to look at Jalen and asked, "Why are you smiling?"

73

JALEN GRINNED SO WIDE HIS FACE HURT.

He held up two thumbs.

"This isn't . . ." The next word was "funny," but Cat's scolding faded as she realized Jalen was signaling a changeup.

After the barrage of fastballs, Porcello was going to try and trick JY with a changeup. It was the perfect pitch, except if the batter knew it was coming. The beauty of it was that the ball would hang in the air like a November apple on a low branch. JY got the signal and turned his eyes on the pitcher at the top of his windup. Everything said fastball, but the pitch came in fat and slow as promised.

74

JY RIPPED IT.

The ball took off, this time headed for left field, over the Green Monster, and on to Lansdowne Street.

The smattering of Yankees fans cheered like maniacs, but they were quickly smothered by a stadium packed with Red Sox groans.

Jalen, Cat, and her mom hugged one another and howled with delight, ignoring the dark looks of the Boston fans surrounding them.

Jalen suddenly froze. "I have to go."

Gregorius crossed home plate, but JY hadn't yet reached third on his easy tour of the bases. Jalen started to push past Cat toward the aisle.

"Wait." Cat blocked him from getting by. "This isn't over."

"JY isn't going to be up again, Cat." Jalen didn't like the look on her face. It was that stubborn look she sometimes got. "They've got the lead. You know that Betances will hold them in the eighth and Chapman will close the ninth. Money in the bank."

"The Red Sox are going to be at the top of their lineup." Cat gripped his arm and tugged him toward his seat. "They could come back and tie this. Anything could happen."

"Yeah, anything could happen." Jalen pointed to the clock. "I could leave now and help smash Chris and the Rockets, that could happen, but not with me sitting here *just in case*. Come on, Cat. JY is gonna be the hero, and I already missed at least an inning, maybe two. I gotta get back."

"I just—"

"You're the one who said 'double play,' Cat. Your words. Tag the bag and make the throw. Something spectacular. Something most people can't do." Jalen threw his hands up. "I tagged the bag, now you gotta help me make the throw. Right now."

In his mind, Jalen was making backup plans. If Cat and her mom wouldn't take him back, he could get a cab, or if he didn't have enough money for that, he could figure out the trains. He didn't want that, though. He wanted Cat with him because he felt like they were a team.

Cat clenched her teeth, and Jalen studied her face to see what it would be.

75

"YOU DIDN'T TAG THE BAG, JALEN. NOT YET." CAT
spoke quietly but with the force of a tidal wave. "You know
you didn't. If you don't get the first out, no one will care
about the second."

Jalen took a deep breath and held it, thinking about
what he wanted to do, and then what he should do. Back
and forth he argued with himself, even though he knew
he'd do the right thing in the end, because that's just who
he was. If he abandoned JY now, when he and the Yankees might need him the most, there'd be no excuse. Not
staying to finish the job he'd agreed to do would be wrong
in anyone's book.

He let out his breath. "You're right. I'll stay, but can we

ask your mom to get the Rover to the garage exit so the instant we know, we can run out of here? Can we wait and listen by the entrance gate, maybe? Then, if we need to, we can run back to the seats?"

"For sure. That's a good idea." Cat wore a smile of relief, as if she'd expected a bigger fight from him. "Mom?"

"Yes," Cat's mom said, getting up from her seat. "I heard you guys. I'm happy to go get the Rover. I'll be waiting right outside like we agreed. We can get right out. And Jalen? I'm proud of you."

Jalen felt his cheeks grow warm, and he looked down at his feet and coughed.

"I'll see you guys in a few minutes. Hopefully." Cat's mom reached over and mussed his hair before she gathered her purse, kissed Cat, and headed for the exit.

Cat and Jalen turned their attention to the game.

Porcello, pulled for a fresh arm after JY's dinger, was replaced by Matt Barnes. Without knowing it, Barnes did everything he could to help Jalen by retiring the next three Yankees in order. Cat gave Jalen's hand a squeeze before quickly letting go. As JY jogged out to second base, he looked over at the two of them and held a thumbs-up against his chest.

It felt good to be acknowledged, but Jalen felt like he had ants in his pants as the inning dragged along.

After a strikeout, Betances gave up a single before Larry Rothschild, the Yankees pitching coach, stopped the action and headed to the mound. Jalen had to grab hold of the bottom of his seat to keep from jumping up and screaming for the coach to hurry. Finally both Rothschild and Betances nodded. The coach trotted back to the dugout.

Jalen looked at the clock on the scoreboard. It read 3:27. Every minute was eating into the Bandits' championship game. "Come *on*."

Betances wound up and threw a belt-high four-seamer. Hanley Ramirez connected and ripped a grounder right at Joe Ros. Ros scooped it up and tossed it to JY like a beanbag. JY jammed his foot against the second-base bag, snatched the ball from the air, and in the same motion, rifled it to first.

"Turn two!" Jalen and Cat were on their feet, shouting and slapping high fives.

The Yankees piled into the dugout.

Jalen bit his lip. "One more inning."

76

THE YANKEES FELL QUICKLY, THREE UP, THREE down, and Jalen began to hope he'd make it for the final few innings of the championship. He had no idea what state the game was in, but he knew the Bandits were good and could hold their own against the Rockets even if Chris had his best day ever.

Cat stood up and said, "Okay, let's get to my mom. If the Red Sox tie it up in this last at bat, we'll have plenty of time to get back to the seats before JY is up again."

They stopped inside the gate. Cat's mom pulled out of the garage and up to the curb when the crowd inside the stadium roared, and the Monster shook beneath the stamping feet.

Jalen looked at Cat, who looked at her phone. "What happened?"

Cat looked up from her phone. "Bogaerts just hit a double."

"Come on." Jalen started for the exit. "Maybe Chris Young will knock one out."

"How about this?" Cat sounded insulted, and she held him back by the arm. "Maybe Chapman will sit the rest of them?"

"Yes," Jalen grumbled. "You're right. That's what I want too, but mostly I just want it to be over."

"I know," she said, not sounding quite so angry. "Trust me. I want you to stomp Chris almost as much as you do."

"You do?" Jalen said.

Cat nodded. "He makes me sick. I hate bullies."

"Well, let's go get him."

"As soon as we know this is over for sure."

Cat's mom motioned to ask what they were doing. Cat held up a finger to her mom and got the radio on her phone, which was better than the app because there wasn't a second of delay, and every second counted. They listened as Benintendi struck out, and Betts grounded out with a short hit to right field that advanced Bogaerts to third.

Jalen groaned. It was now 3:51, and even if they left

now, he'd likely make just the final two innings. If Ramirez knocked in Bogaerts without scoring himself, they'd go into extra innings and he'd likely miss the entire championship game.

The Red Sox radio play-by-play man, Tim Neverett, set the stage, drawing out all the drama of a 2–2 count with Chapman trying to seal the win against their archrivals, ending it against arguably the Red Sox's most potent batter. Before Neverett could get the words out over the radio broadcast, they heard the stadium erupt in cheers. A split second later came the call.

"Ramirez swings and he got it! This ball is high and long and headed down the line for the Green Monster, Bogaerts is headed home, and it is . . . it hits the wall and—oh my! Oh, my, my, my!"

Jalen slapped his hands against both legs and leaned forward, growling at the radio. "Tell us! Tell us what *happened*!"

77

THE STADIUM ABOVE THEM ROARED.

"Joe," said Neverett to his analyst, Joe Castiglione, "I've never seen anything like *that* before. Reuben Hall launches himself one foot, two foot off the corner of the wall and makes the *catch*, and this game is over, folks, in dramatic fashion, 2–1 Yankees."

Castiglione laughed bitterly. "There was a ball girl in 2009, Tim, who did something just like this, *just* like it, and it makes me wonder if Reuben Hall saw it himself on YouTube and just said, 'Hey, if a ball girl can do it, then so can I.' Amazing . . ."

"Ha-ha!" Cat squealed, and turned and slapped high fives with Jalen. "Yes, yes, yes!"

"Come on." Jalen raced through the gate and they threw themselves into the Rover.

"Mom, go!"

"Yes, all right." Cat's mom put the Range Rover into gear and the SUV jumped into the street.

They took a right, then a left, and surged up Brookline. Jalen looked back behind them and saw waves of people streaming from the stadium. He looked ahead at the empty road and giggled. "This is so great, Mrs. Hewlett."

They went right onto Route 2, then left onto Charlesgate, without any traffic at all. Jalen knew the fields were just fifteen minutes away without traffic. They raced around the ramp that led to Storrow Drive, flying now because Cat's mom knew that for Jalen, every second counted. They whipped around the tight bend so fast Jalen swallowed hard, because an accident was the only thing that could stop them now. Suddenly Cat groaned. A snake of red taillights stretched along Storrow Drive.

"Mom, can you go back?"

The traffic in front of them was stopped completely.

"Maybe I can back up." Cat's mom put the Range Rover into reverse and looked into the mirror before she stopped. "No. I can't."

Jalen looked back. There were several cars stacked up behind them now on the ramp. In front of them some drivers had gotten out of their vehicles for what was apparently a total shutdown of traffic.

"How far are we?" Jalen asked Cat.

"Three miles straight up the river," Cat said.

Jalen swung open the door, the trees and the river and the skyline blurred by tears, because he did the math quickly. First, he'd never run three miles at one time. Second, even if he could make it without collapsing, it would take him at least forty minutes, and by then the game might just be over.

"I'll meet you guys there," he said before he closed the door, thankful for the sunglasses that hid his watery eyes.

Cat got out too, and followed him as he set off running down the ramp, his baseball cleats clacking against the pavement. They climbed the guardrail, stumbled down a grassy slope, and fell in with a throng of runners, walkers, and bikers along the wide riverside path.

Cat was right there alongside him until she suddenly pulled up short and grabbed Jalen's arm. "Wait."

Jalen looked toward the traffic, thinking that maybe it had begun to move, but Cat was looking the other way, toward the river, when she said, "I've got an idea."

78

ONLY CAT WOULD HAVE HAD THE NERVE AND THE
confidence to walk right up to the water's edge and hail
the Harvard women's crew boat, waving with both hands
and shouting, "Ahoy! Ahoy there! Yes! You! Please! We
need your help!"

Two female coaches in shorts, Harvard women's crew
T-shirts, and boat shoes looked at each other. Their
expressions were a mystery beneath the shade of their
visor brims, but they shrugged before steering closer.

"Thank you! Thank you!"

Jalen wasn't sure how much the women planned on
helping, or if they were just curious as their team rowed
on without them toward the bridge, but Cat leaped onto

the flat bow of the boat before they could protest, then turned immediately to Jalen, waving him on as well.

He hesitated, but then jumped when Cat barked, "Jalen! Now!"

He landed at the edge of the platform and wheeled his arms to try and keep from falling back. Cat grabbed his Bandits uniform and tugged him firmly aboard, then turned back to the amazed coaches and spoke like a machine gun. "We have to get to Harvard Stadium as fast as you can take us. Jalen needs to get to a championship game that's more than halfway over. We just came from Fenway, where he was helping the Yankees—you might even recognize him, the Calamari Kid who helped save James Yager's career—but there's a traffic jam, and I could tell just looking at you two that you'd understand that burning desire that all athletes and coaches share to do everything you can to win . . . and I *knew* you'd help."

One of the coaches frowned and said, "You can't just jump on our boat. We've got practice here. We—"

But the other coach cut off her counterpart with a wave and a bubbly chuckle before she said, "Grab hold. We'll have you there in just a few minutes. You're right, I love a winner."

Off they went, surging up the river with a breeze in their faces.

Jalen leaned close to Cat, and her hair tickled his face. "'Ahoy there'? Where'd you get that? *SpongeBob*?"

"It worked, right?" Cat shielded her face and smiled, her eyes sparkling almost as much as the sun on the water.

Jalen laughed. "Yes, it did."

They passed the team's boats, called shells, with the girls working arms and legs like the pistons of an engine and their coxswains' steady chant through their megaphones. "Stroke, stroke, stroke . . ."

The head coach raised her bullhorn and turned it toward her team. "We'll be back, ladies! Chivalry is not dead!"

Jalen hunched his shoulders. "Oh, brother. Chivalry? That's for knights and maidens. Do I look like a maiden?"

"Relax," Cat said. "It's a modern era. Women can be chivalrous too."

"If you say so, Cat. I know better than to argue with you, even though Daniel might."

"I wonder how he's doing." She pointed up ahead as they rounded the bend. "Look, the stadium."

The crew coach pulled up to shore well short of the stadium and said, "You'll have to walk up the ramp there so you can cross the bridge. Good luck!"

Cat shook the coach's hand. "I'm a Harvard Crew fan for life."

The coach laughed and waved as they jumped ashore, then reversed the boat and headed downriver. Jalen and Cat took off, up and over, past the stadium built in the image of the Roman Coliseum, and skirted past the hedge that served as the outfield wall for the main field.

The first thing Jalen saw was the Bandits' black-and-gray uniforms in the home team dugout. The next thing he saw was the scoreboard out behind left field, just over the hedge and beneath the lowering sun. The Bandits were down 1–0, and it was the top of the sixth and final inning. Gertzy was on the mound with one out. Dirk Benning stood at the plate, looking serious and mean, with the scrunched-up face of a troll baby.

As Jalen and Cat marched toward the dugout, Gertzy threw a high fastball that Dirk took a cut at. The Rockets player caught hold of it late, and the ball zinged foul, right over Jalen's head. Because they were following the ball, Dirk, Chris, and the entire Rockets team saw his approach. They all seemed to snarl at once.

"I'm going to sit in the stands. My mom just texted that it was an accident, but they cleared it and she's on her way. JY's on the way too, so I'll sit with them." Cat quickly walked away.

Jalen didn't have time to do anything but blush and keep going.

Daniel was in right field, and when he saw Jalen, he shouted, "Yo! Rockets! Your powder's gonna be wet now! Baseball Genius is in the house!"

Jalen pulled his shoulders back and marched into the Bandits' dugout.

"Jalen, you decided to show up." Coach Allen's voice and face were hard to read.

Jalen didn't know if his coach was joking and happy to see him, or annoyed and bitter that he had arrived so late. He looked at the coach's eyes for a hint and tried to communicate everything he'd done to get there without speaking.

"This team has been playing its heart out," Coach Allen said, "but your buddy Chris has been killing us. Look at him. See him grinning at us?"

"He's not my buddy." Jalen gritted his teeth. "I busted my butt to get back here, Coach. I want a piece of him. I want to wipe that smile off his face."

"So, now you're here, you want me to pull someone *out* of the lineup so you can get a piece of this guy?" Coach Allen frowned and tilted his head. "Because you've got his number. Yes?"

Jalen held his chin high. "Yes."

79

COACH ALLEN BROKE INTO A SMILE. "WELL, THAT'S music to my ears, son. Get yourself warmed up. We're at the bottom of the order, but I've got an idea."

Out on the field, Gertzy struck out Dirk, and the Rockets player pounded the ground with his bat and yelled at the umpire, "That was *terrible*. That was *awful*."

"Awful!" Coach Gamble ran out of his dugout and kicked the third base line, sending a puff of white chalk and dirt into the air before retreating back to the dugout without even looking at the umpire.

"The worst call I've ever seen!" Dirk scowled at the umpire.

"You want to finish this game, or hit the showers?" The

ump glared at Dirk, who disrespectfully turned his back and walked away, cursing to himself.

"Two outs." Coach Allen pointed as Chris swaggered up into the box. "But your 'not buddy' was the one who got their run. Put one of Gertzy's fastballs out of the park in the second inning. Practically hit that building."

Jalen looked past the outfield hedge across the parking lot at the big brick building. "He's big."

"And good, too." Coach Allen looked at his score book. "He's not afraid to use that curve, and we just can't hit it. Fanny took a walk in the fourth, and Gertzy hit a single, but otherwise we haven't had a sniff. When we do connect, they're dribblers."

"Well, I hit him in Little League, and in practice, too," Jalen said.

"That's what I'm hoping for." Coach Allen put a hand on Jalen's back. "We ended the last inning with our first two batters, so Fanny is up. He's our number three, then Gertzy is cleanup. You'll bat five. I figure if those two know the pitches, at least one of them can get on and then—if we hold here—you could get us on the board and win this thing. It'd be a good day for you to do it, because not only is the Harvard coach watching, someone said Yale and Princeton are here too, so . . . you can never start impressing people too soon."

Jalen looked into the stands and swallowed, thinking he'd probably rather not have known about the college coaches. He saw Cat sitting alone and gave her a little wave. The crack of a bat turned his attention to the field. Chris ripped a line drive over second base and stretched a single into a double when the center fielder bobbled it. Chris hopped up and down on the bag and hooted and hollered, pumping a fist at his teammates, who jeered at the center fielder, shouting, "Hey! Dribbles!"

"These guys are pretty low on sportsmanship," Coach Allen said with a frown.

Jalen saw that the next batter was Caleb Paquet. He burned at the thought of how Caleb had thrown a beanball at him to get in with Chris and Dirk.

"What do you think? Is Gertzy too worn down, or do you like him to finish this?" Coach Allen was talking, and Jalen wasn't sure if it was to him.

"Are you asking me?"

"You're the genius, right?"

"He can get them," Jalen said, knowing it was what he hoped, not what he knew.

Caleb got behind on a 1–2 count before he blasted one of Gertzy's fastballs toward the right-field hedge.

Jalen's stomach plunged.

Daniel took off at a full sprint, hit the track that ran

along the inside edge of the hedge, and leaped into the air, reminding Jalen of Reuben Hall's amazing catch at Fenway. Daniel twisted in the air, stretching, and snagged the ball, but was immediately swallowed up by the hedge.

80

THE ONLY THING THEY COULD SEE WAS DANIEL'S glove.

He held it up high, even as the hedge trembled and shook while he wormed his way out. Once he was free from the greenery, he reached into his glove and held the ball up for everyone to see. The crowd broke out in applause. Daniel got halfway to the dugout before he bowed dramatically to the bleachers and the Rockets dugout, then tossed the ball to the umpire and joined his teammates.

Daniel hugged Jalen. "You're just in time, amigo. You must have carefully planned it this way."

Jalen could only laugh at that.

"What?" Daniel squinted at him.

"I'll tell you later," Jalen said before he turned to their coach and started to tell him about the signals he'd use to help his teammates.

"All right, guys, listen up!" Coach Allen barked at the team, and they fell silent so everyone could watch Jalen, especially Gertzy and Fanny, who'd be up first.

"Chris has only three pitches." Jalen showed them the first sign, four fingers. "This is for his fastball; he uses that the most. Then this is for his curve—it's a *C*. Two thumbs up is his changeup, because if he throws that and you know it's coming, it's a real meatball."

"Anything else you can tell us?" the coach asked Jalen.

"Yeah." Jalen nodded. "When it's a curve, you'll know it's coming, so don't get nervous. Just swing early on it— before it drops too far—and you'll pull it into left field for a base hit. Don't try to kill his curveball, just hit it."

"You guys got that?" Coach Allen stared around at his team's faces. Many wore looks of disbelief. "This is the real deal, what he's saying. Jalen can read the pitches. Now, everyone bring it in. We practice like champions, and we play like champions, because we *are* champions. Let me hear it, on three, *champions*, one, two, three . . ."

"*CHAMPIONS!*"

Their fists went up, and Fanny headed for the plate.

"Let's go, Fanny!" they shouted. "Fan-ny, Fan-ny, Fan-ny . . ."

Chris looked over from the mound and patted his big butt. "I got your fanny right here."

"That's enough!" the umpire shouted, then addressed Coach Allen. "Coach, come on. There's kids in the stands."

"Ump, that's his name. His name is Fanny."

The umpire shook his head like he didn't quite believe it, but he put his mask down and shouted, "Okay, let's play ball!"

Jalen knew Chris well, and he didn't hesitate to hold four fingers up for Fanny.

Chris wound up and in it came, a fastball, low and down the middle. Fanny let it go.

"Strike!" The ump turned and pointed to the side like a big leaguer.

"What?" Fanny began to complain until Coach Allen shouted his name in a voice so stern it chilled Jalen's backbone.

Fanny looked at Jalen, and Jalen now wished he'd told Fanny not to be so obvious, but there was nothing he could do about that now. He shifted his attention to Chris. He saw the curveball and made a *C* with his hand. Fanny nodded and stepped into the box. Chris wound up and in it came.

Fanny swung hard, missing it entirely.

The Rockets players burst into cheers and jeers.

Fanny's face twisted up in rage. He bit his lower lip and stayed in the box.

Jalen knew the fastball was coming, and he held up four fingers, but Fanny wasn't looking. He was glaring hatefully at Chris and crowding the plate. Jalen knew what was going to happen before it happened.

Without thinking, he shouted, "No!"

But it was too late.

81

JALEN WASN'T SURE IF FANNY DID IT INTENTION-
ally or not, but his fierce look and his toes touching the
rubber of home plate sent Chris off the deep end.

Enraged, the mini-ogre threw his fastball right at
Fanny's head.

Instead of ducking, Fanny stood tall.

The ball hit his helmet with a popping sound the crew
coaches might have heard out on the river. Fanny went
down like a sack of potatoes and the helmet rolled off his
head. The Bandits players howled with rage. Coach Allen
and Coach Miller—who was coaching third base—bolted
toward home plate, crying foul as they went.

Coach Gamble and Coach Benning were out of their

dugout too, shouting their best excuses for Chris's actions. "That kid crowded the plate! That was a good pitch!"

The Bandits coaches dropped to their knees beside Fanny, who sat up shaking his head as if to shed a bad dream. He wasn't staying down, even when his coaches tried to get him to relax. Fanny grabbed his helmet from the dirt and dusted it off as he jogged to first base.

In the confusion, Jalen wasn't sure how many people heard what Fanny said to Chris, but Jalen heard it clearly. "Thanks for the free ride, you meathead."

Chris growled and took two steps toward the baseline.

Fanny held the helmet on his head and scooted the rest of the way to first, putting distance between himself and the giant pitcher.

"Coach, your guy is okay, and he was crowding the plate," said the ump in response to Coach Allen's outcry.

"You're sanctioning a beanball?" Coach Allen's face was bright red, and he stabbed his finger toward the pitcher's mound. "That kid should be *ejected*!"

Coach Gamble cupped his hands around his mouth and shouted from just outside his dugout. "Sit down, Coach! Let the umpire ump, you coach . . . if you know how."

"If *I* know how?" Coach Allen clenched his fists and took a step toward the other dugout.

The umpire's hands went up. "Coach, get back to your

dugout, or you'll forfeit this game right now."

"*I'll* forfeit?" Coach Allen wore a look of total disbelief, but he did as the umpire said and returned to the dugout.

"Let's go," said the ump. "Batter up."

Jalen tugged on his batting gloves, picked up his bat, and went to the on-deck circle, where he could loosen up while he helped Gertzy.

Gertzy walked to the plate and had a stare-down with Chris.

Jalen signaled curveball, knowing that Chris wanted to show his rival pitcher all his stuff.

It was a beautiful curveball; it came in low but dropped even lower and tailed off to the outside of the plate. Gertzy didn't have to swing. He shouldn't have, but he did.

"Strike!"

Jalen signaled four fingers next, and Gertzy nodded.

The fastball came in way high, but Gertzy swung again, popping it foul up and over the backstop.

Chris grinned. He had a huge advantage, and he had his batter swinging. Whatever pitch he threw, Jalen knew it wouldn't be anything good. But then Chris did something probably no one but Jalen saw. He straightened his backbone and looked briefly into the stands and gave his cap the slightest of tips toward Cat. It was in that instant that Jalen knew Chris had changed his mind. He was like a tom turkey and he wanted to fan out all his pretty feathers on display.

Jalen dropped his bat and signaled two thumbs up to Gertzy, a changeup, a meatball.

Gertzy gritted his teeth and set his feet.

Jalen's heart galloped.

Part of him wanted Gertzy to put one over the hedge and defeat the Rockets in grand style, but another part of him hoped for something less, because Jalen didn't want to win the game just with his mind. He wanted to win it with his own arms and legs and bat, too.

He could only watch as Chris wound up and threw with what looked like all his might. But Gertzy knew, and Jalen knew, the ball had been in the palm of Chris's hand, and it had no spin, so it came in slow. Gertz swung big, but he topped it, sending a ground ball zipping through the gap between first and second. The right fielder moved up on it, but Fanny was already at second, and Gertzy was safe at first.

Jalen gulped and clutched his bat. Daniel was beside him now, ready to take over the circle.

Jalen's friend gripped him by the shoulders. "You got this, amigo. This is all you. It's what you do. Hey, what's that faraway look, dude? What are you thinking?"

Jalen forced a smile. "Be careful what you wish for."

"What?" Daniel scrunched up his face.

"I'll tell you later." Jalen turned and marched toward the plate.

82

JALEN'S MIND TOOK OVER.

Everything was suddenly calm and clear. He didn't want
to have to knock one out, because if Chris was smart—a
thing in question—he'd throw nothing but curveballs and let
his defense win the game. Jalen wanted to move the runners
into scoring position, and he knew just how he could.

Jalen stared hard at Chris, stared him right down
until he saw the fury in Chris's eyes. Then he stuck out
his tongue, just for a split second, so that no one but
Chris would think anything of it, but Chris knew. Jalen
scratched his butt and faked a yawn, then stepped into
the box, crowding the plate.

He knew he couldn't get Chris to throw another beanball.

Even Chris knew he'd be kicked out of the game, but he did send a fastball over Jalen's head so high and so hard it crashed into the backstop. Fanny and Gertzy took off.

Dirk's mask flew through the air, and he scrambled for the passed ball. Jalen thought Fanny might try for home plate, and he did, rounding third base at full speed. Jalen stepped back. Chris raced forward from the mound to cover home plate. Dirk got a handle on the ball and zipped it to Chris. Fanny slid face-first. Chris caught the ball on the run, stretched out his glove, and dove.

The ump hovered over the cloud of dust and hesitated before he jagged his thumb. "You're out!"

Chris was on his feet and cackling like a madman and slapping high fives with Dirk.

"How'd you like that? *Fanny.*" Chris turned to Jalen. "You're next, Little Orphan Annie."

Chris stalked off toward the mound. Jalen knew Chris was referring to his missing mom with the insult, and it hit home. He thought of Chris's other insults from the past, and he thought about the destroyed sandwiches his father had worked so hard to make and been so proud of, and he ground his teeth.

The tying run was still at third, but now Jalen was the winning run, and he knew it was all or nothing.

Everything Chris did, Jalen expected. His ability was in

high gear, to the point where he almost felt like he'd been here before. The first pitch was a lousy curve, so low it hit the dirt. It was a brilliant play by Dirk not to let it past him.

It was a 2–0 count, and that gave Jalen some breathing room. From the dugout, Chris's father roared, "Chris! You settle down! Settle down right now! This kid cannot hit you! Just do your thing!"

Chris's angry look eased up a bit, and he nodded toward his father.

Jalen looked up into the stands and saw Cat, now sitting with her mom as well as JY. He felt a flood of pride and determination as he stepped up to the plate.

Chris threw a nasty curve, but it was low and outside, so Jalen let it pass.

"Strike!"

Jalen turned in disbelief but then clamped his mouth shut and focused on Chris. He was still ahead in the count, 2–1.

He saw another curve, just as low and outside as the last one. He did a quick calculation and swung, barely ticking it so that Dirk was able to catch it.

With a 2–2 count, Jalen knew that Chris would try another curve to sit him down.

Going through Jalen's mind was the kind of hit he could get off that curve. If it was an obvious strike, he'd

do his best, but he still believed the pressure of throwing all those curveballs would make the next one an errant pitch, too low and too outside for the ump to call it. Jalen hoped the ump owed him a call after that last one.

Jalen readied his bat. Chris wound up and let it fly.

The spin told Jalen he was right about the curve. He wasn't certain about the accuracy. It would be close.

He let it go by.

The ball snapped into the catcher's glove, and Jalen turned to the ump, who paused before barking, "Ball!"

Jalen warmed with relief.

It was a 3–2 count.

That count, and Jalen's refusal to swing, he knew, would tempt Chris into throwing his best, hardest, fastest pitch. Chris didn't want to risk a questionable call by an inconsistent ump, but even more, Jalen knew that Chris wanted to see him swing in futility, like a dying man's last gasp of breath. Chris wanted to embarrass him, wanted to *hurt* him.

It would be a burner, right down the middle. No question about it being a strike.

Chris peeled his lips back off his teeth like a jackal over a carcass, wound up, and threw with every ounce of hatred he possessed.

In a blur, the pitch rocketed toward Jalen.

83

JALEN REARED BACK AND PUT HIS ENTIRE BODY
into it.

He hit the ball on the sweet spot and blasted it into left field, right over the hedge.

He dropped the bat and raised his hands in the air but didn't shout out. He wanted to win with class, so he dropped his hands and set off around the bases, soaking in the cheers from the stands and his dugout. When he crossed home plate, though, his team was waiting for him. They knocked him down with hugs and piled on. Daniel pulled him out from under the mountain of laughing boys and hugged him, lifting him into the air before everyone settled down to shake hands.

Neither Chris nor his dad would look at Jalen as they passed through the line, but Jalen didn't care. In a way it made things even better.

After the trophy presentations, Coach Allen raised Jalen's hand like a heavyweight champ. His team mobbed him again, and then Cat, her mom, and JY appeared.

"I'm so glad you made it." JY hugged him. "And I appreciate all your help at Fenway."

Jalen couldn't stop grinning.

Cat's mom hugged him next, then Cat, holding him long enough for him to feel that it was something different before they separated and she looked into his eyes. "I am so happy for you, Jalen. It was the ultimate double play."

"Thanks to you."

"Well," she said, "you deserve to have your dreams come true."

She hugged him again, and Jalen didn't think anything in the world could ever be better, until he felt a tap on his shoulder and turned around.

84

THERE SHE WAS, TALL AND UPRIGHT, WITH SKIN
as dark as those enormous eyes. She was elegant and majestic, wearing an electric-blue dress with an inky black flower pattern. Her cheeks had lost some of the roundness he'd seen in her picture so many thousands of times, but the thinner face made her cheekbones more pronounced, reminding Jalen of Cat's mom.

He knew who she was. She didn't have to say it, even though she did, and the words were the sweetest sounds he'd ever heard.

"Hello, Jalen. I'm your mother."